I0624625

Published by Kadath Press

Goderich, Ontario, Canada

cameron_straughan@yahoo.com

www.cameronstraughan.com

Second Printing – August, 2020

ISBN: 978-0-9686981-8-1

Q: Do you live your life?
A: Only when it's around me.

... from a dream I had.

More Praise for Neurotica

"4.0 out of 5 stars. Clever and fun. I've always enjoyed short stories, as sometimes I want to finish a story in one sitting. In this collection there are 16 stories in just 100 pages; some of the stories are only a page or two. The writing is very clever and at times laugh out loud funny. I didn't find these stories neurotic, more the stuff of very interesting dreams or told by someone under the influence of hallucinogenic drugs. If you are looking for something different this would be a great choice--it was a fun read."
-- Amazon Review

"I like the cleanness, point of factness and absurdity of your style. You write as though nothing could be more logical than the illogical events you describe. I have grown to have considerable affection for your naive narrator."
-- Tim Lander NANAIMO PUBLISHERS CO-OP

"The writing throughout 'Neurotica' is clean and precise, which effectively counters/compliments the fantastic elements of the prose. If you like your fiction soaked in the unusual, look into Straughan's enigmatic world."
-- Matthew Firth BLACK CAT 115

"Each story has a Twilight Zone quality to it, often ending with a punch line that hit me like a cream pie in the face. Straughan is a writer committed to disseminating his unique vision and it's clear that, with each new anthology he produces, his work gets stronger and more engaging, and I enjoy watching that growth. Kadath Press offers you a rare glimpse into the mind of one of Canada's most interesting surrealist literary talents. Don't miss out on the opportunity!"
-- S.R. Duncan RAIN CITY REVIEW

"Neurotica is full of surprising moments, and its absurd and funny style is a refreshing departure from a lot of other work that takes itself too seriously."
-- Jennifer LoveGrove WORD

NEUROTICA

CAMERON A. STRAUGHAN

ACKNOWLEDGEMENTS

Thanks to all the fellow writers and publishers who have given me support, advice, and constructive criticism over the years. A special thanks to the late C.F. Kennedy for instilling in me a passion for independent publishing and - most importantly - for encouraging me to keep on writing.

CONTENTS

The Life of a Thinker 1

A Walk in the Countryside 5

Submerged...8

During the Lunch Hour 16

The Flame..20

A Call to Duty 24

Headliner 30

"It" – Monster from the Unknown....................................52

The Trial 58

How to Keep Cats Out of Your Garbage..........................67

The Future, a Radio, and a Travelling Salesperson 68

A True Story About a Monkey 74

Rumours 75

As the Crow Flies 77

A Note on Fancy Toffee Tins 89

The Package 90

The Life of a Thinker

The thinker wanders the streets alone. The curious bulge in the left pocket of his jacket keeps people at a distance. He doesn't display it often; only to those he trusts the most - only those who can tolerate it.

Entering a grocery store and recognising someone he thought he knew well, the thinker makes a slip - a momentary lax in reasoning. They rush down the aisles and out the doors, leaping counters and grabbing what food they can, amidst the sound of cars screeching away from the parking lot. Broken glass, toppled shelves, and abandoned shopping carts are left in their wake. The thinker, feeling defeated, picks up the device and puts it back in his pocket. He shuffles out of the deserted store.

Wandering the streets aimlessly, or so it seems, the thinker attracts undue attention. Pedestrians move to the opposite side of the street. They find something repellent about his left pocket. They do not approach him regarding this; they do not want to. Fear drives them away. Only at a distance do they feel comfortable. The thinker does not understand this (the device is just not meant for them).

Seated in a cafe, surrounded by familiars, the thinker is barely aware of what's being said, but not because of ignorance. He shakes his head, straining to listen. He tries not to draw attention to himself, but it's hard for him to jump in at any given moment. With a handkerchief, he wipes the blood from his neck, shoulder, and clothes; some of it begins to run down his arm. He cannot enjoy the music, because of the sound of drilling. His body besieged with spasms, his face winces and contorts.

The device is now firmly attached to the left side of his head. With its tendrils wrapped around his face, obscuring his immediate view, it begins to burrow deeply, through his ear, and eventually into his brain. Mixing, pumping - swirling round and round in a clock-wise fashion. The thinker is caught up in the flash of images. His familiars try to console him; it is only part of human nature to try including every one.

"You're rather distant," they might begin. Or perhaps: "That's a nice shirt you have there."

When the thinker has an attack like this, he is prone to seek solitude. He learned at an early age that it is best. The device operates more efficiently in privacy, with no excuses necessary to explain a sudden lack of social grace. More importantly, the thinker seeks solitude because he is concerned about his familiars.

He does not like the look on their faces, as he falls from his chair, writhing on the floor in pain. Teeth clenched, shaking all over, he suffers great distress, because of their forced nonchalance. Glancing up at the ceiling, they keep talking, to save his dignity, as if they could never be embarrassed or inconvenienced. What good actors they are. He claws at the tendrils covering his eyes. The sound of drilling fills the small cafe, causing his familiars to speak loudly to one another, in order to be heard. He appreciates their performance, dedicated to him. But he fears he is over-working them. He has forced them onto a tightrope of understanding, teetering between dislike - fostered by misunderstanding, of course - and a vain will to help him, although at times it seems impossible.

"Pay no attention to me," the thinker cries out in pain, hoping to be heard above the device, "I'm all right down here."

At times, he wished he had their support, to help him up off the floor, but ultimately he goes without it. It is his fault, of course - partially due to stubborn nature, partially force of habit. He tries in vain to pull himself up, clinging to the back of a customer's chair. The blood, now a pool around him, causes him to slip back onto his stomach. The customer takes one look at him and turns back to his coffee, not wanting to get involved.

"Sorry to disturb you," the thinker hisses between clenched teeth, the pain quite extreme, "enjoy your coffee."

Yes, the thinker is often distracted in such a manner, but he is always sincere and apologetic, never wishing to harm anyone. He looks up, noticing a waiter trying to pass by with a tray of orders.

"Sorry about the mess," he waves his hand feebly, the waiter carefully stepping over him.

It is unfortunate, but much of the thinker's life is composed of incidents like this. Once and awhile, however, he meets someone who is willing to open themselves up to such an experience, regardless of the consequences. This is a rare event - to be cherished. Not many can bare the pain and live to tell. The device is not forgiving. It allows no escape once it has you; its tendrils are steadfast, its drill-bit long and viciously curved.

So maybe the thinker shouldn't condemn those who fear the device. He tries his best not to. He does not know what their lives are like, so he cannot rightly comment. But they know what *his* life is like. They see the pain and suffering, the misunderstanding, the futile attempts at making contact with others, and the device itself. Yes, maybe they are happy without the device. Yet, it is surprising that more have not been affected by it. It has an affinity for people forced together, by circumstance or intention. For example, if seated side by side, it can jump from one person to another. For this very reason, the device is highly unpopular at church gatherings.

With bibles open, donations ready, and in best attire, the congregation listens carefully to the minister. Everyone is silent, of course. Only the minister's voice carries throughout the church. They hang on his every word, punctuating each sermon with 'amen'. And when he forgets the words and compensates by mumbling, they hang on his every mumble, punctuating prolonged mumbling with 'amen'. The beloved flock, peaceful and tranquil, with the sound of mumbling lulling them into a feeling of security and comfort on a sleepy Sunday afternoon. Suddenly, a cry fills the church, followed quickly by another. The flock turn their heads back and forth in unison; there is a general feeling of subtle wonderment amongst them. Another cry, and then the sound of someone falling to the floor, kicking about madly.

"What's that racket in the back row?" the minister cranes his neck, setting down his bible. "Is someone thinking for themselves?"

The alarm is sounded immediately. Ushers rush to the back row. Before anyone can be distracted from their feelings of detachment and malaise, the thinker is hauled off the ground and dragged out of the church. Without further incident, the mumbling continues.

Back on the street, wandering aimlessly, or so it seems, the thinker is once again a victim of his surroundings. People stop and stare; some race to the other side of the street. Maybe some of them envy the thinker for diverging slightly from the norm; although it is debatable what the norm really is, since the very powers that determine these standards can't be familiar with the sort of pain the thinker goes through. Such thoughts give the thinker a headache. The device is full of joy. It celebrates this joy by crawling out onto the thinker's sleeve, for all to see. For a moment, the thinker is proud of himself. But he can only wear his heart on his sleeve for so long, before it crawls back into his pocket.

A Walk in the Countryside

At times, those things viewed from a distance don't appear the same under closer examination, particularly if expectations are high. This was the case during one of my many visits to the countryside.

Strolling along an isolated gravel road, something caught my eye, far ahead, on the opposite side. There was a black umbrella and beneath it sat a young lady in matching dress - a stark contrast, set against the fields of golden wheat stretching into the distance. From what I could make out at such a distance, she had a very fair complexion, which explained the umbrella. She appeared to be reading something, pausing only to sip at some beverage that was at her side. It was quite a novel scene and I was intrigued, to say the least. Why had she chosen such an odd place to sit and read? Was she awaiting a ride? I made up my mind to speak to her when I drew close enough; after all, it would be rude not to, seeing that we were the only people around for miles.

As I drew nearer, shyness overcame me. I found myself staring at the gravel, unfolding beneath my feet. When I figured I was close enough, I prepared myself to speak, looked up from the road and turned towards her. However, much to my dismay, the umbrella, and the young lady beneath it, turned out to be nothing more than a small turnip floating four feet off the ground. I was both puzzled and embarrassed, as I approached it. How could I make such an error in judgment? Perhaps I should have my eyes examined, I thought; but optometrists rarely test for this kind of thing.

It was so obvious, now that the turnip was directly in front of me - sometimes hovering up to eye level. I nervously shot a glance up and down the road. How would I explain this, if someone was to pass-by and see me? I wanted to leave - to avoid undue scrutiny or further embarrassment - but at the same time I was unable to; this floating turnip had a strange magnetism. I was about to reach out and touch it, when I heard the roar of an engine behind me. Startled, I stepped away from the turnip, unable to think of a quick explanation for my being there. A large truck rumbled to a stop, and three men fell out. The truck seemed to be in better condition than they did, which wasn't saying much for the truck. One of the men carried a butterfly net; the other two had evil grins on their faces. I noticed that the back of the truck was full of turnips. No doubt, they had been all over the countryside, collecting. I quickly realized their intentions.

I had been to many places, and experienced many things, so I knew this floating turnip was rather special. Reaching up to the top of my head, I discovered I was wearing a large bowler hat. I didn't question its presence; one shouldn't question such things if they are beneficial. I took off the hat and placed it over the suspended turnip. Grasping the brim, arm outstretched, I lead the turnip away, with the intentions of taking it home. The three men did not attempt to stop me; I gave them a serious look that convinced them the turnip and I were leaving together. They looked puzzled, and somewhat defeated, as I walked the turnip into the distance; never would I let it fall in to their hands.

The long walk home proved to be tiresome, but amusing nonetheless. With my arm outstretched, carefully guiding the turnip hiding comfortably beneath my hat, I received many friendly responses from passers-by who thought I was tipping my hat to them. By the time I reached the small cottage I had rented, the entire countryside considered me the most cordial person alive, which wasn't entirely true.

With the turnip inside, I began to doubt my intentions. How would I explain this to my parents? Mother told me recently to avoid turnips and concentrate on my work. However, that seemed hypocritical; when I was young, she told me turnips were good for me. Feeling quite proud of myself, nonetheless, I called a friend over.

Coming in through the front door, he saw me seated, smiling, on the sofa, the turnip floating just above my right shoulder. He began to shake his head.

"You're so predictable," he said, bending down to untie his laces.

He sat down directly across from me and lit a cigarette.

"I suppose you're going to rub this in," he spoke between puffs; "you've always had a strange kind of luck with things like this."

"It's funny," I began, in an effort at relieving his envy, "I didn't know what to think at first," I paused, glancing up at the turnip, "but it has an odd manner that appeals to me."

"You look good together," he admitted.

"The benefits go far beyond that," I felt obliged to add; "I won't have to pay to get it into the theatre!"

Submerged

After closing the door and turning off the light, Jonathan stepped across his bedroom floor with great care. He did not wish to step or slip on anything that could be - and probably was - littered across the floor of his personable bedroom. Of course, in the absolute darkness, maintained through some effort on the part of the curtains and blinds, this was no easy task. But he was completely familiar with his surroundings. Even if he was walking on his hands with his eyes plucked out, he could still successfully find his comfortable bed.

The bed, consisting of a simple mattress on top of a box spring, creaked and moaned when he finally fell upon it, as if it had been reluctantly awakened from a pleasurable dream. It had been another laborious day for him - studying, reading, walking, staring at the sky. He decided he must fall asleep quickly, if he was going to make the most out of the evening hours and awaken in the morning to face another stressful day.

He tried switching his position several times, in a desperate attempt to invite sleep. Every time he did so, the mattress would express its dissatisfaction - groaning, as usual. The mattress's complaints served only to drive sleep further away from his tired limbs. He tried to adjust his blankets, but ended up wrapped in such a complete cocoon he could no longer move his legs or arms. He feared he might asphyxiate himself, or gangrene might set in. In either case, he would be unable to wake up on time. He could not tolerate that.

After a brief, rather one-sided struggle, Jonathan was soon free. He lay motionless, much to the satisfaction of his cantankerous mattress. Staring upwards at the veil of darkness surrounding him, his eyes closed almost unconsciously. Concentrating on the screen provided by the inside of his eyelids, he watched the dance of pale blue and green lights. Some appeared as planets, some as stars, others as fantastic macroscopic organisms of some unknown origin. It was then that he felt himself drifting off to sleep.

His body began to undulate gently, his mattress floating

along. He could hear the waves breaking against the side of his bed. The summer heat was gone. In its place, the refreshing ocean breeze. He sat up in bed and opened his eyes. Although he could not see for the darkness of his room, he reached over the edge of his bed and immersed his hand in the cool, swaying waters. Suddenly, something strange seized him. So incredibly pale, it was luminous. He had no chance to pull away. It had clasped him like a mother clasps her child at the carnival. He was quickly pulled beneath the waves.

Jonathan had very little time to contemplate what was happening to him. Everything was a blur. Water rushed over him. His senses were awash with fear and anxiety. He prayed he would not drown. Opening his eyes, all he could see was the pale, luminous hand, clenching his wrist. This hand, its point of attachment nowhere in sight, was dragging him down into the abysmal depths of the ocean. Struggling was futile. The grip was too tight and the water rushing past made movement impossible, or sluggish at best.

Although he could see nothing - aside from the hand - he was aware that the depth was rapidly increasing. The pressure had reached the point at which his head ached terribly. The salinity became so high that his eyes burned and his taste buds screamed in agony. Further down through the black ocean depths, he could not help but think that the person who had seized hold of him must have incredibly long arms - about five thousand feet long. But still, he could not see those arms; only the hand was visible.

Amazingly, Jonathan had not yet drowned; in fact, he felt a strange sense of immortality. Yet, he wished his strange ordeal would soon end. The pressure began to give him a severe migraine, his bladder felt as if it would let loose, and the steadily increasing salinity was unbearable as well. A slight chill overcame him, probably because his pyjamas were quite thoroughly soaked.

Just as his fears reached their apex, his downward journey ended. Bursting out of the water, he landed amongst silk pillows and satin sheets. He felt as though he never made that harrowing journey through the ocean depths. Miraculously, he was completely dry. He was, however, completely disoriented. Had he just been pulled upward through the water - in which case he had surfaced and landed on dry land - or had he really made a forced decent into the ocean, as he initially thought? The confusion stirred his curiosity.

With some reluctance, because he was strangely afraid of what he might see, he raised his head from the receptive silk pillows. He attempted to stand up when the top of his head suddenly became immersed in water. In a state of shock - the likes of which he never experienced before - he fell back down onto the pillows. Touching his hair to see if it was possible, he turned a startled glance upwards to confirm his fears. The ceiling above him was formed by the deep ocean water which he just passed through.

Jonathan's disbelief was such that he had to reach up and touch the ceiling with his hand. With a quick stroking movement, he splashed the water hanging above him. The resulting droplets of water did not fall onto the pillows and sheets he knelt upon, as would be expected on the account of gravity. Instead, they rose back up to rejoin the ocean water forming the ceiling.

It became painfully obvious to Jonathan that he had become trapped within a three foot high crawlspace of some sort at the absolute bottom of the ocean depths. The very water he had been pulled down through formed a lid to his cage. But at least he now had air to breath; he was thankful for that.

All Jonathan wanted to do was go to bed. Now he was in such a predicament he did not know what action to take. He decided to survey his confines, for lack of any plan of escape (after all, how could anyone swim upwards through thousands of feet of water?). He had to do this on his hands and knees; he was so tall that if he stood up the ocean water suspended above him would engulf him from the waist up.

The first thing he noticed, upon looking around him, was the lack of furnishings within his deep sea prison. Only several silk pillows and satin sheets covered the floor. He was also struck by the hypnotic dance of bluish light that seemed to radiate from the rippling ceiling above him. The silk pillows and satin sheets - all of them white - were made strangely luminous by this light.

Upon further surveillance, he discovered that a wall of beautifully formed corals of every colour imaginable seemed to encase him in what appeared to be a circular area with a diameter of approximately twenty feet. Of course, this was but a mere estimation on his part. He did not have the necessary equipment to take proper measurements with. Nevertheless, the situation did not look promising. So far, it was obvious he was trapped within a small area at the abysmal depths of the ocean.

His fears of confinement quickly left him. A noise came from just behind him. Gripped by fear, his limbs reduced to an immobile state, his crouching body was forced to strike an even stranger pose.

"Hello," a feminine voice flowed into his ears, like a soothing lullaby.

Jonathan dared not turn around, even though the voice seemed warm and friendly. He could not imagine who on Earth could be sharing his strange confines with him. He felt foolish. How could he have possibly overlooked the presence of someone else? Had this person - a young lady, no doubt - been behind him all along?

"Hello?" the voice came again, as if Jonathan had misunderstood what was said the first time.

At the risk of being rude to his guest - or his hostess - he began to turn around slowly, not knowing what to expect. When his eyes fell upon the other occupant, he became so startled he leaped up and almost drowned himself upon hitting the ceiling.

"Who are you?" he gasped, pushing back his saturated hair, wiping the water from his face.

There before him lay the most beautiful creature he had ever seen. In literature, he had never encountered such beauty. The goddesses of Greek mythology were all put to shame. He had never seen her likes in the thousands of films he had seen. Her hair was as black as the priceless oil which pulses, like blood through veins, within the deep ocean floor - untouched by mankind. Her eyes were equally dark. Her fair skin was made luminous by the hypnotic blue light, cascading down from the ocean ceiling. A thin, almost transparent material was draped over her, subtly hinting at the ethereal shapes contained within. She appeared to be quite tall - taller than average. Of course, this was but mere estimation on his part. He did not have the necessary equipment to take proper measurements with.

"Who are you?" he asked once again; after all, she said 'hello' twice, so he felt justified for repeating himself as well.

"I am a culmination of all of your hopes, dreams, and

desires," she replied, with a hypnotic voice. "I am both beautiful and intelligent, both honest and trustworthy, and even if there was someone else down here with me, I would remain faithful to you."

"But how will you and I escape from here?" Jonathan stirred, filled with a sudden sense of urgency.

Even though he was overwhelmed by the beauty of the young lady stretched out before him, part of him was still contemplating a means of escape.

"Escape?" the young lady smiled, looking up at the ocean which formed the ceiling above them. "There is no escape - there is no need for escape. You will remain down here with me. We will live together in complete happiness. You and I will have no use for the contrivances of the upper world. There will be no work to be done only pleasures to be explored. We will not need any food, water, or other furnishings besides silk pillows and satin sheets. We only need each other down here, and we will remain here - together - until the end of time, and just beyond that."

At that point, Jonathan seated himself amongst the silk pillows, massaging his temples in a desperate bid to escape the confusion of his predicament. He briefly looked upwards, noticing several highly unusual species of fish swimming through the pristine blue waters of the ceiling. These deep sea fish were equipped with a dazzling array of luminescent organs which they used, with great skill, to lure prey into their massive, gaping jaws. He closed his eyes, put a hand to his forehead, and began to shake his head in disbelief.

"Oh what a task I've chosen," he moaned. "Why can't things be easy for me?"

"What do you mean?" she sat up, apparently surprised by his comment.

"I can't stay down here!" he motioned with his hands.

"Why not?" she sank back down. Her soft, friendly voice seemed to have vanished. Her dark eyes lost their liveliness, only to be replaced with disappointment.

"Well, I'm already feeling claustrophobic down here. Let's face it," he paused, shaking his head, "I'm just too tall. I can't stand up at all down here for fear of drowning, and I'm already starting to get back aches from having to crouch over."

"Well then, I will massage your back for you," she smiled,

gracefully crawling towards him.

"No thanks!" he pleaded, raising his hands. "If you touch me, I might be tempted to stay."

She stopped advancing towards him. Her perfect composure now escaped her. She stared down at the silk pillows, tears collecting in her haunting eyes.

"Then you really don't like me?" she sobbed. "You don't find me attractive?"

"No, I think you're very attractive - extremely attractive," he attempted to console her. He felt great sympathy for this beautiful and most likely very lonely young lady, now reduced to such a state. He reached out and touched the soft, luminescent skin of her shoulder. Yet upon doing so, he was filled with such unusual sensations that he thought he had better keep to himself before losing sight of reason.

"I would really like to get to know you," he continued. "You strike me as an interesting person, but it would have to be under different circumstances. This just won't do." Too shy, and perhaps too nervous to face her directly, he glanced around at the deep sea confines he shared with her.

"I really thought you would stay here - with me," she shrugged. "I thought you'd like it here. I thought this is what you wanted."

"It is an extremely tempting offer," he tried to explain his position, without further upsetting her, "but I'm afraid that I cannot accept. Besides, we'd probably get tired of each other, if we remained down here, in this little room, until the end of time."

She looked at Jonathan as if he was speaking a foreign tongue, tears still rolling down her cheeks. She embraced herself, as if suddenly embarrassed by having presented herself in such a stimulating manner.

Jonathan felt awkward, to say the least. He wondered if he was making the right decision. Half of him was a realist and wanted to return to the surface. His other half preferred to stay far below the ocean and live out all of his fantasies with the intoxicating beauty who lay weeping before him. Finally, he reached a compromise.

"Maybe we could keep our relationship going through correspondence," he suggested.

"I don't have an address. I don't even have a mailbox," she sobbed.

"Well, what if I call you sometime?"

"Do you see a telephone down here?" she wiped a few tears from her exquisite cheeks. "No lines service this area."

He was at a complete loss. How could he bring happiness to her without having to compromise his freedom? He definitely did not want her to feel unwanted, or rejected; she did seem to encompass everything he ever wanted. To leave her so soon would seem impolite, if not insane.

"I'll tell you what," a suggestion quickly came to him, "I'll stay down here with you for a little longer. We could talk awhile."

"For how long will you stay?"

"About ten minutes."

The young lady burst into new fits of crying. Jonathan had not expected her to react like that to his suggestion. He felt like a complete ass for placing such limitations on their relationship.

"I'm sorry," he reached over to comfort her. "I do not wish to torture you, or make you unhappy, but you must understand that I cannot stay with you much longer, even though part of me longs to be with you. I have a lot of work to do in the surface world - studying, reading, walking, staring at the sky ..." he paused briefly. He was ashamed of the grief he had brought to this wondrous person. "I suppose that it is best if I just leave now."

She seemed more at ease, now that he'd given her a loving embrace. However, the embrace had the opposite effect on Jonathan. It filled him with ecstatic delight, which he tried to conceal. Suddenly, an important question arose.

"How do I get out of here?" he gazed up at the rippling blue ceiling.

The young lady gracefully motioned with her delicate hands. A whirlpool formed just above him. Somehow, he knew what he had to do. By leaping into it, he would be transported back up to his bedroom. Yet, he hesitated and turned to her.

"Will I ever see you again?" he asked, with true feelings of remorse at having to leave.

"Yes, as a matter of fact you can - if you still want to," she replied, hoping that he would follow her advice. "I will always exist in your dreams. Deep down inside, your memory of me will remain intact, so you will always know where to find me."

"Then I will look for you there."

"I knew you would," she smiled, her tears vanishing. "You're unlike other men. They're all too wrapped up with reality, but you're always day-dreaming and fantasizing so much that you hardly ever get any work done."

They joined together in a good laugh, although he did not know whether she had just paid him a compliment or not. With some reluctance, he rose to enter the whirlpool above him. He took one last look at her, still lying across the silk pillows and satin sheets. She was smiling now; he was glad of that. Her dark eyes were every bit as hypnotic as the bluish light, cascading down from the ceiling. He felt like tasting her lips as a final farewell. But if he was to do that he would surely go mad with pleasure. To avoid further temptation, and since he had gained her respect, he leaped up into the whirlpool.

The journey upwards through the ocean depths was much easier than the forced decent he had originally experienced. Travelling within the whirlpool, he managed to stay completely dry. In what seemed to be an incredibly short period of time, he was propelled from the bottom of the ocean to the surface. Flung from its churning waters, he landed safely on his bed, which immediately expressed its dissatisfaction at his return by issuing a tremendous sigh.

Without further interruption, Jonathan fell into a deeper sleep. Yet, when he awoke in the morning, he felt as though he had not slept at all.

During the Lunch Hour

I was alone in a restaurant - my lunch half finished - when I received a sudden visit from an angel. I'm not sure where he came from. Well, of course he came from Heaven - everyone knows that. But I'm not sure where he was previously hiding. Perhaps he was sitting in a dark corner, out of view. Maybe he had a waitress seat him near a window where the light flooded in - angels are fond of that sort of thing. Maybe he was fluttering overhead. At any rate, he was beside me, and I regretted my ability to attract such eccentrics when I didn't want to be disturbed.

Not wishing to be rude, I pretended to be absorbed with my meal, when in fact I was blatantly ignoring him. However, this strategy proved to be quite a chore. He made things very difficult for me. He kept peering over my shoulders. His glow reflected off my cutlery, blinding me. He beat his wings. Feathers flew up and around me, falling onto my plate. I began to sneeze; he was wearing too much Old Spice. Quite suddenly, he stepped back and began a kicking motion. His foot flew up, just inches from the side of my face. With my spoon suspended before me, I rolled my eyes. Slowly I turned my head, not wanting to be kicked.

"What are you up to?" I frowned.

"I'm trying to knock your hat off," the angel replied.

"But I'm not wearing a hat."

"Well, now that I have your attention," the angel set down his tray and slid into the seat right next to me.

At that point, I really didn't know what to do. Obviously, I couldn't ignore him, yet I simply *had to* finish eating. Staring down at my meal, I was barely aware that I held the attention of almost everyone in the restaurant. Suddenly, a wing flew up in front of me.

"Sorry about that," the angel shrugged, as I pulled back, "it's a nervous tick."

"There you are," the waitress smiled, coming towards us. "I thought you were still over by the window."

"No, no," the angel laughed, "I moved over here."

"Here's your milk," she set the glass down in front of him.

"Thank you."

"Now," she pulled out her pad and pencil, looking at us both, "is this all on the same bill?"

"Yes," the angel nodded, "I'll take care of it. Thank you."

"You two enjoy your meals now," she winked, turning to leave.

The angel moved in closer to me.

"Tip monger," he whispered, "thank God we're rid of her."

"I really have to be going," I finally spoke up, taking another mouthful of chips, "I don't have time to talk."

"This won't take long," the angel patted me on the shoulder. "I have very little to say. I'm more of an observer than anything - not a talker. I could sit off to the side and watch people forever - just like you."

The angel paused, a wide grin on his face. He watched me shovel spoonful after spoonful of chips.

"You're making me nervous," I frowned; "it's ruining my digestion."

"I know something that you don't know," he smiled.

"Oh really?" I sipped my water. "And you're an angel - what are the chances?"

"That's right," he slapped my shoulder. "I know all about your life."

"I've got an important meeting to go to," I wiped my face with a serviette. "Did I forget to mention that?"

The angel just laughed and shook his head. Sighing, leaning on the table, I decided to humour him. Besides, he struck me as a persistent type who might go on to bother me at weddings, funerals, and future lunches, if I didn't get it over with right there and then.

"Allow me to illustrate," he sat back, sensing my interest. Pen and notebook suddenly in hand, he drew a single short straight line. Smiling, he displayed it to me. Needless to say, I was more impressed with his ability to make office supplies appear at will than his talent as an artist.

"Is that it?" I laughed.

"What do you mean?" he looked at his sketch and then back at me. "I worked long and hard on it!"

"But that can't be me," I laughed, pushing my plate aside,

leaning back in my chair, "and I can give you a good reason why not."

The angel frowned - my own favourite pastime. Shaking my head, chuckling to myself, an incident came to mind, one of the more recent ones, which would prove him wrong.

"Take this morning for example," I shrugged, "I was rushing to get downtown for a job interview, which is why I'm rushing to get my lunch over with. Stepping onto the number eight bus, I noticed it was completely empty, which was very unusual for that time of day. Regardless, I went to pay my fair and that's when the driver, who was of obvious Viking descent, caught my attention. He was not the driver I was accustomed to. I asked him a few questions about the usual driver, but he just looked at me blankly. Leaning in closer, I noticed that his ears were plugged with ants. He spoke up, telling me that he rarely got invited to picnics. Confused by this, I wondered if it would interfere with getting to the job interview on time. Suddenly, the driver had some sort of fainting spell and fell over the wheel. The horn sounded and the parking brake came loose. The bus started to slowly roll down the street, the horn blaring. With the door still open, I decided to seek alternative transportation. I hopped off the bus and hailed a cab. Now here I am!"

The angel stared at me, squinting somewhat. His wings twitched ever so slightly. He crossed his legs, leaning against the table. Rubbing his chin, he looked around the restaurant and shook his head.

"What the hell kind of story was that?" he shrugged.

"Exactly," I laughed. "Now let me see that illustration of yours."

Slowly, perhaps reluctantly, he handed me the pen and notebook. Barely able to contain myself, I flipped to a new page. To the best of my ability, I sketched a circle, and handed it back to him. I burst out laughing at the expression on his face. All eyes turned towards us - if they weren't already. I don't know why I laughed so hard; perhaps it was just the playful absurdity of it all. But the angel, obviously insulted, took the notebook and quietly left the restaurant.

Shortly thereafter, I left the restaurant. Outside, the angel was nowhere in sight, but I couldn't care less. My thoughts were elsewhere. However, I was extremely upset that he left me with the bill. Stepping out onto the street, pulling on my jacket, my mind adrift, I didn't hear the horn roaring towards me. A moment later, I was struck by a runaway bus and killed instantly.

And now, out of lack of anything better to do, seated in a far corner by the window, where the light comes in, I have penned this tale, from beginning to end. I see a young fellow sitting alone, nervously gobbling down his lunch. When my glass of milk arrives, I think I'll go over and bother him.

The Flame

I struggle to extinguish the flame. It has burned for too long, and my eyes and fingers ache from turning the pages in front of me. I must press down on the book and the table, so the waves can't carry it all away. Only the chair I'm sitting on is truly secure. Luckily, I'm not wearing anything of value. I'm soaked to the skin. I picked a poor place to relax and read. Just then, the chain around my leg grows taut. She's climbing up from the ocean depths, using me as an anchor. I've waited on shore just long enough for the lava to become stylish furniture for onlookers. They're in the hot seat now. All of this is none of their business. But then I'm the one airing his laundry in public. I've never felt so clean, as the ocean crashes against me. Holding my breath, I lose sight of my pen and notes. The chair and desk float up to the surface. No doubt, the spectators will fight over these souvenirs, as they wash ashore. The chain prevents me from joining the furniture. Otherwise, as I wash ashore, one of the spectators might be tempted to take me home as well. Together with the chair and desk, I'd make a good companion piece for anyone's den or study, providing, of course, that I was fed, and dusted, on a regular basis.

She is still pulling herself up from the depths. It is impossible to tell, however, whether she is pulling herself up or I am being pulled down. I lose some stability with each tug on the chain. I have even more trouble trying to extinguish the flame now. The candle floats and bobs in the current. My hands are sluggish in the deep, salty water. Fish gather around, but not with the hopes of collecting some furniture. Swimming up beside me now, she takes the candle in her hand. I can barely see her in the darkness of the ocean depths. Licking the tips of her fingers, she extinguishes the flame. All light is gone.

Suddenly, we are bound together and swirling round and round at the county fair. This is our favourite ride for drying off our clothes, although it often makes me nauseous. The onlookers are below us. They've got my chair and desk. One sits and reads my notes, stopping only to squeeze the water out of them. One of them doodles absent-mindedly. They look good with my furniture. I'm jealous, I must admit.

"Don't bother with them," she kisses me lightly on the forehead.

"But my notes, and my schedule," I argue, "in the hands of complete strangers!"

"Don't let it distract you," she laughs, "just enjoy the ride!"

The ride is making me dizzy, as usual. So often we've done this - too often. Why can't we just lay side by side in the sun to dry off? Or why bother wearing heavy wool clothing at all? Round and round we go. It costs us both £ 1.25 a piece. It probably would have cost the same to have our clothes dried at the launderette, but not if we put our clothes in together. I'm quickly becoming bored with the monotony of this routine. I try to convince a passer-by to throw me a book. It's difficult, spinning round and round on adjacent rides, for two people to exchange books. He finally throws one that I can catch. All the rest have fallen to the onlookers below. No doubt, they are seated at my desk, enjoying each one. I look at my book: 'An Existentialist's Guide to Housekeeping with a Pictorial History of the Tea Pot and Notes on the Taxonomy of Molluscs'.

"Damn," I cry, "I read this one last week!"

"Are you into the books again?" she starts, holding me tighter still.

"Of course not," I lie, "I only wanted to humour the fellow who kept tossing them my way."

Like a lion, winter falls upon us. She becomes silent; that look is in my eyes, more in the left eye than right, because a good quantity of snow has obscured my vision during the ride. We both know that this nonsense must stop. We're too mature, and it's too cold for such games. So we both decide on it; our paths will be determined separately. Leaving things up to fate, we step off the ride and win an ocean cruise for two.

The cruise is an enjoyable experience - like we were never apart - aside from the fact that we are once again bound together by various types of rope, a family portrait, and various ornaments from the kitchen, all of which I am forced to carry in my backpack. We soon accept a different view of things than other passengers. We don't expect it, or plan for it, but I suppose that it's inevitable. Through some lack of foresight on the crew's behalf, we aren't booked into a cabin proper, but are kept tied together *beneath* the boat. It is a glass bottom boat, so all the passengers can gather in the main ballroom and watch our every expression. Sleep is impossible, but we look so clean, as the water rushes past us and the boat roars along. At cocktail hour, all we see is the bottom of patented leather shoes, the spikes of high-heeled shoes, billowing dresses, and the odd cigarette butt falling from some drunkard.

I recognize some of the guests; to my surprise, they are the typical onlookers. They bring my table and chair out onto the dance floor and insist on remaining there for a better view. Much to my chagrin, I notice wads of chewing gum stuck to the bottom of my desk. What a nuisance they are. Everyone is forced to dance around them. One of the onlookers, busy at my desk, suddenly leaps up and demands that everyone remain quiet so that he can finish reading my diary. Regardless, the passengers spend most of their time dancing; they're all sick and tired of watching us, surging in the water below the boat. We've become commonplace to them. Only the elderly janitor pays any real attention to us.

He is a kind man, who waits for all the passengers to leave so he can mop the ballroom. In the meantime, he is making sure that the glass separating us from all the festivities above is devoid of any smudges or smears that would interfere with our view. When there is a lull in the dancing, he lays newspapers out on the floor, so we can catch up on current events. Feeling playful, he does a comedic tap dance routine, directly above us, with his mop becoming his willing partner. The sound of his shoes on the glass is barely audible to us, because of the water rushing around us, but we swear that he seems to be communicating with us. If this is the case, we have no real idea what he is trying to tell us, although it is obvious that he is, at best, a mediocre dancer.

We know no other lifestyle, admittedly. Vacations like this do help somewhat. We return home feeling cleaner than ever. We go through a lot of wool clothes, though; they always shrink. A perfect fit is always hard to find; you're rather limited when you're being dragged through the ocean.

Leafing through volumes and volumes, the vacation photos appear like pressed leaves. Each of them a piece of time, connected to one another by branches, all nourished by the same system of roots. Some fall out of place, only to be received somewhere else. With age, they might disappear forever. We spend many afternoons in the living room, flipping through memories. The current, always persistent, insists that the pages keep turning. Smiling, gazing down at the captured moments, she gets kelp stuck in her hair. How beautiful she is, kelp or not. Recollection is our main recreation, I suppose. Television offers little relief; reception is poor; the passing of a whale overhead interferes with both television and radio reception. But the place is clean, especially the kitchen, although cooking is a chore. We have great difficulty keeping the pilot light going. Needless to say, we eat a lot of salads. They always taste too salty; we both agree on that.

Life in the depths is difficult, but I am anchored there, we both are. With great effort, I return to the shore to work, but lazy sunbathers take undue notice as soon as they see me pop out of the water with my desk, chair, candles, books, and notes. I've always hated undue attention. It won't be long before she's pulling at my chain again anyway. But I don't mind; she has a way with candles.

A Call to Duty

It was 6 o'clock in the morning, when I was awakened by a call from the Prime Minister. He asked me to come to London right away, but on the way over I was supposed to go door to door, collecting funds for new government programs. So off I went - hastily dressed, barely awake, hardly thinking, hungry, but full of a sense of duty.

Several hours later, after visiting at least one hundred homes, I realised the difficulty of my situation. Why hadn't it occurred to me earlier? I felt like a fool. What was I doing, going door to door at such an early hour? Worst yet, how could I be sure that it was actually the Prime Minister who had called me? I began to suspect I'd fallen victim to someone's idea of a practical joke. But on the bright side, I had collected just over one thousand pounds, so who got the last laugh?

I was considering taking the money and flying to some place exotic, when I saw someone far up the street, running towards me. I immediately felt guilty. Did I really think I could keep the money? Did I really think he'd let me away with it? Of course not! But how did he know? How did he know where to find me, let alone the intentions I had adopted?

Soon he was standing before me - the Prime Minister, in his shabby blue housecoat, brown dress socks and matching penny loafers. He was gasping for air, sweating profusely, and puffing on a large cigar. No doubt, he'd been running for quite some time.

"How are you doing?" he asked, expecting me to be professional, even under such strange, almost impossible circumstances.

"I've collected just over one thousand pounds," I was sure to add emphasis, *"for the government programs."*

"Yes, of course," the Prime Minister laughed, shaking my hand, *"the government programs.* And I've collected quite a bit myself."

Clenching the cigar firmly in his teeth, he fumbled through the pockets of his housecoat and pulled out two crumpled wads of banknotes, amounting to no more than a hundred pounds.

"And I got this cigar!" he was quick to add, posing with it.

Needless to say, my initial impression of the Prime Minister was not strong. I wondered if his government programs would be any better; one could only hope so. Regardless, my sense of duty was definitely becoming a thing of the past. The Prime Minister, of course, seemed oblivious to the look of disappointment and frustration I had developed. Rubbing his chin, puffing on his cigar, he gazed skyward, apparently caught up in his own thoughts.

"You know," he waved his cigar at me, pacing back and forth, "your technique is much better than mine, on the account that you've collected a lot more money than me - almost ten times more! You've definitely caught my interest, young man. I'm glad I called and got you out of bed."

"Isn't London a long way off?" it suddenly occurred to me, wanting to get this business over with as soon as possible. "We should probably catch a plane, or something."

"No need," the Prime Minister shook his head. "You're doing so well. Let's see how much more we can collect, while they're still willing to give!"

Reluctantly, I approached the next door. The Prime Minister paced by the curb, smoking his cigar. I rang the doorbell. Almost immediately, I heard a heavy-set person coming to answer. The door jerked opened. A large, bearded, barefoot man in a black T-shirt and blue jeans stood before me.

"Yes," he said gruffly.

His size and intimidating tone caught me off-guard. I almost forgot what I was going to say.

"I'm collecting money this morning," I chirped, "money to help fund new government programs. Are you interested in donating a few pounds?"

"New government programs, eh?" he leaned against the door frame, looking me up and down.

I knew immediately, under his scrutiny, that he wasn't going to give me a single penny. I got the impression he thought I was pulling his leg - and I had disturbed him at such an early hour! I wanted to apologise and turn away, but I was rooted there, unable to look him in the eye. I had never felt so uncomfortable. I waited for him to send me on my way, or worse, accuse me of running a scam. However, I soon realised that I was not the object of his scrutiny after all. He was leaning forward, looking at something *behind* me. Instinctively, I turned around. The Prime Minister was waving at us from the road - puffing his cigar, tightening the belt of his housecoat.

"Well then," the man fumbled through his pockets, "here's a fiver."

With the government coffers now five pounds richer, the Prime Minister and I were off to the next house.

"I want to observe your technique up close, this time," he followed closely behind me, as I approached the door; "I find it fascinating!"

"It's simple," I prepared to knock. "I just politely ask for the money."

"Wow," he shook his head. "Who'd have known it would be this easy? And the guys told me this idea would never fly!"

I knocked on the door a few times, before a frizzy-haired woman appeared in a flowery dress. She seemed very suspicious, refusing to open the door all the way. Seeing the Prime Minister behind me, she automatically assumed I was with the government.

"What is it?" she asked, giving me a dirty look.

"I'm collecting funds for new government programs," I spoke up, trying to remain friendly and enthusiastic. "Are you interested in making a donation?"

"No, absolutely not!" she screeched. "I don't approve of your organisation, or your collection methods! Don't try to pull the wool over my eyes. I hear all about your government on the news, and I know better than to get myself involved with something like that. Now beat it - both of you!"

The door slammed shut. The Prime Minister and I left quietly, almost speechless, somewhat embarrassed by the incident. We moved on to the next house, hoping for better luck; there was little else we could do. At the pathway leading up to the front door, I stopped and turned to the Prime Minister, trying to be polite about it.

"Maybe you shouldn't be standing right behind me when I knock."

"You're probably right," he nodded. "I'll wait by the curb."

I approached the front door, feeling much more confident,

now that the Prime Minister wasn't breathing down my neck. He seated himself comfortably by the road, pulled his housecoat over his legs, and puffed his cigar in silence. I knocked a few times, before hearing a voice slowly approaching the door, begging my patience. The door opened rather hesitantly, and an old man greeted me with a smile.

"Can I help you, young fella?"

"Good morning," I beamed, glad to encounter someone in good spirits, "I'm collecting money for new government programs. Would you care to donate anything?"

"Weren't you just here?" the old man called out, looking towards the Prime Minister, still seated on the curb.

But the Prime Minister did not answer, letting on he was admiring the houses across the way. I was confused, and embarrassed, to say the least. I should have known that, judging by his attire, the Prime Minister was lacking in organisational skills. Otherwise, we would not have bothered this old man twice in one morning.

"Your friend was already here!" the old man pointed towards the Prime Minister. "Must have been here ... oh ... about an hour ago."

"Sorry to inconvenience you," I apologised quickly, but the old man wouldn't let me off that easy.

"It's like I said before," he roared, "I'd be willing to donate something, if only I had a proper pension! And let me tell you, I worked my fingers to the bone for years! Now you have the nerve to come here and ..."

Suddenly, the Prime Minister grabbed my arm and pulled me away.

"Let's press on," he directed me towards the next house.

"Have a nice day!" I called out to the old man, still lecturing about his pension from the front porch.

The Prime Minister dragged me around a corner.

"That man said you already visited him," I ventured, somewhat upset that the mistake was made at my expense.

"Yes, sorry!" the Prime Minister smiled, straightening my collar. "I wanted to see if *you* could get anything out of him!"

As you can imagine, with the Prime Minister's busy schedule, there was no time for my grievances - or anyone else's, for that matter. He was soon using his effectiveness as a diplomat to get me up to the next door, or maybe it was just the fact that his brown penny loafers had better traction than my black dress shoes; when he pushed me from behind, I slid along quite nicely. Reluctantly, I knocked twice and almost immediately heard young feet racing to answer.

"Hi there," I greeted the young girl, dressed as though ready for school, "I'm here with the Prime Minister and we're collecting money for new government programs. Is your mum or dad home?"

"Mum, dad," the girl cried towards the kitchen, "some guy's at the door with the Prime Minister."

"Ask them what they want," her father hollered back.

"He wants to know what you want."

"Tell your dad we're collecting money for new government programs," I smiled patiently.

"They're collecting money," the girl cried out again, "for new government programs."

"Who is it at this hour?" her mother came into the kitchen, getting ready for work.

"It's some guy with the Prime Minister," her father set down the paper. "They're collecting money. Have you seen my wallet?"

"You're actually going to give them something?"

"Sure why not," he searched around the kitchen, finally finding his wallet. "It's not easy going door to door, especially these days. Times are tough."

The little girl, leaving the Prime Minister and me waiting at the door, ran back into the kitchen.

"You give this to the man, honey," her father gave her a five pound note, returning to his seat.

The little girl, overjoyed, full of purpose, raced back to us.

"That was stupid!" her mother reprimanded her father, too busy with her briefcase to bother seeing who was at the door. "How do you know it's really the Prime Minister?"

Her father paused for a moment, slid his chair over and peered down the hallway towards the front door. He saw the Prime Minister in his housecoat and brown penny loafers, puffing his cigar, standing alongside me, and his little girl presenting us with the five pound note.

"It's him all right," he turned back to his paper.

"Here you go," the little girl handed me the five pounds.

"Thank you," I smiled, "have a good day at school! Bye now!"

"What a lovely family," the Prime Minister examined what little remained of his cigar, as we walked away. "It's good to know that people can still afford to have children."

Unfortunately, that was the last successful canvassing experience we had. It proved to be a bad time for us; everyone was heading to work - those who had jobs. The Prime Minister became frustrated, his cigar finished long ago. Some people saw us coming up the street, no doubt tipped off by neighbours we had visited, and immediately turned off all the lights, pulled the curtains, and locked the doors. Yes, the Prime Minister just wasn't a popular fellow to share a morning walk with. I actually found myself feeling sorry for him. He looked so defeated, in his shabby blue housecoat and clashing penny loafers. His brown socks only added to the pathos. He insisted that we head into a cafe for a late lunch. Although he previously showed me a large wad of banknotes, he now claimed to have no money whatsoever, so I had to spring for the bill; but it was canvass money anyway.

The Prime Minister quite suddenly decided to head back to London, having had more than enough excitement for one day. He hailed a cab and took the money I had collected.

"Take me to London," he leapt into the back seat of the cab.

"London?" the driver was shocked. "You got money?"

"I do now!" he roared.

The cab sped off into the distance. I was left with no money to get myself home. Walking all the way, I arrived back at my flat just past dinner time. Being somewhat tired, to say the least, I decided to go straight to bed. But this time I made sure my telephone was turned off.

Headliner

When Christopher was young, his father taught him to keep his head above water. Now he was putting that lesson to good use. Yes, that time had come, in his mid-thirties, when everything piled up and he felt lost in the current. Money drifted by, yet he was powerless to seize hold of it; most opportunities were lost to him. Yes, economics were a problem. Countless forms and legal documents floated in and out of his life, the burden of the common man. The wind played havoc with family photographs. Memories of the wedding dissolved before him. Alas, the sufferings of a married man. The unrelenting waves broke against him, drenching his hair. His temples ached from the cold ocean water. His lips tasted salt, eyes stung, and a storm was brewing on the horizon. All the while bobbing around on the horizon.

Although Christopher was surrounded by forms, documents, money, and photos - the flotsam and jetsam of his life - he could not locate their source. Not only did the waves obscure his sight, but, strangely, he had no control over his limbs. In fact, he felt an uncomfortable numbness from the neck down; almost a lack of presence, as if he wasn't quite there. Maybe he really wasn't. How else could he explain it? After all, it was a miracle that, with no effort on his part, he managed to keep above the water. Of course, no effort was possible.

He was troubled by his situation; he could not recall how he arrived there. Perhaps the initial fear of his predicament was so overwhelming that he forgot everything prior to it. Maybe that was it. With the storm brewing and all, his mind had been adrift - hardly a mood for piecing things together. Yes, like walking around a corner, daydreaming, and running into someone, or absent-mindedly descending a staircase, suddenly twisting an ankle, he was shocked into the reality of his situation. He would have to accept it, pure and simple. He was lost at sea, paralysed, but not yet drowning, and it was as simple as that.

But the sudden realisation troubled Christopher nonetheless. No amount of rationalizing could relieve his frustration. Where was his salvation? How long had he been bobbing around at sea? With no celestial bodies in sight, due to the impending storm, he had no sense of direction. He was truly lost. Instinctively, he cried out, even though there was no evidence of anyone around to hear him. Yet, his own cries gave him comfort that he *was* actually still there, still fighting the odds stacked up against him.

"If a man cries out in the ocean, does anybody hear?"

Why did he ask himself that question? He worried the same madness might claim his conscience, having already claimed his memory. But maybe his memory was erased by some sort of drug, the same drug that paralysed his entire body, leaving him with a sickly feeling of loss, as if the water was flowing right *through* him. Could it be true? Had there been some sort of conspiracy set against him? By whom? Suddenly, he heard a familiar sound, or at least he *thought* it was familiar. Maybe his memory hadn't completely failed him after all. The sound came again, in the near distance, hidden by waves and a darkening sky. It disturbed him, that sound. He didn't know why, but he loathed it. Yet, at the same time, if he could turn and head towards it, he would. Salvation at last, it occurred to him. He began to scream at the top of his lungs, providing they were still there. Again the noise. A distant ringing it was, followed by a burst of laughter; he could hear it all clearly now. Although the ringing seemed familiar to him, he could not recall, try as he might, why it filled him with such contempt. And then it drifted into view.

It was a long greyish shadow with a few illuminated portholes, massive smokestacks silhouetted against the brooding sky, waves breaking against it. The engines seemed to be off, so he could hear the ringing all the more clearly, the laughter as well. Not normal laughter, but sinister somehow; as if someone was enjoying something forbidden. Christopher's sense of hearing was so acute he could pick up all of these nuances.

"Help me," he cried up at the ocean liner, hoping it wouldn't pass him by, "I'm over here!"

Thunder rose in the distance. The wind seemed to pick up, tossing Christopher mercilessly. The forward deck was in view, as the ocean liner towered over him, threatening to pass right by, or run him over; either fate was not preferred. He thought he saw someone on the deck, racing back and forth, like a chicken in a storm, or, more aptly, like a chicken with its head cut off. There definitely was someone there! Christopher tried to call up to the person, but he swallowed some water, the waves becoming more savage, and the winds carried his words astray. Coughing, gasping for breath, gathering the strength to call out again, Christopher noticed that the person on the deck, high above, was tossing garbage overboard. Box after box flew skyward, twisting in the wind, spiralling downward, floating around Christopher, landing on his head, mocking him. It wasn't just garbage, he realised. It was photos, documents, and money, all swirling around him now. His realisation was immediate. He had come to the source.

Christopher was angry, to say the least. All his belongings were being thrown overboard, cast out to sea for some unknown reason. Hardly a good policy for a reputable ocean liner, if that's what it was. He intended to report the incident to the Captain as soon as he got on board. Of course, that was his main concern - getting on board.

"Help me," he called out again, regaining his breath, "I'm paralysed. Please help me!"

The ocean liner seemed to be passing him by. There was no other sign of life on the decks, aside from the person tossing things overboard, too busy with his work to hear Christopher far below, apparently. Christopher recalled that, from a distance, some of the portholes seemed to be lit, but under closer examination, they seemed vacant, lifeless. He was crying out in vain at a towering piece of steel, cold and impersonal, drifting right by him. Suddenly, a light at the end of the tunnel, in the shape of a dimly lit porthole, slowly drifting towards him in the darkness. He saved his energy, preferring to call out at that crucial moment when it was passing directly overhead. He could hardly contain himself. The waves bouncing off the ocean liner seemed to be pushing him away. The porthole was almost directly overhead; he became transfixed, almost speechless. Their eyes seemed to fall directly upon each other, despite everything. Her face was perfectly framed in the soft light. Stunned, he screamed something unintelligible, almost uncontrolled.

"Christopher?" she cried against the wind.

She snapped her porthole shut and raced out of her quarters. Was he saved? Did she see him - hear him - amongst the darkness and the waves? The porthole he spotted her at passed into the distance. Soon the stern would be passing by, and then he'd be left in the wake, alone, helpless. But the alarm rang out again and again, and two people raced to the railing of the aft deck. They struggled in the wind with a long pole, trying to get it over the railing and down to Christopher. He would be saved! But the rescue plan, as it unfolded before Christopher, was plagued with logistical problems. For one thing, the two rescuers aboard the boat had great difficulty getting the pole anywhere near Christopher; and another, Christopher, being paralysed, could not take hold of the pole, or the ridiculously small net, which he noticed at the end of it.

"I'm paralysed!" Christopher screamed, in desperation, hoping to be heard. "I can't take hold! You'll need something else - a bigger net!"

"Did you hear that?" the ship steward shot a glance at the first officer, who was trying to stop the bell from ringing. "He says this won't do!"

"Well it'll just have to do," the first officer scowled, straining to direct the pole towards Christopher, far below.

The wind was merciless and the bell was just getting in the way now. Ringing on and off erratically, the first officer no longer found it so enjoyable. The initial excitement was always a lot greater than a prolonged engagement made necessary by a stubborn sense of duty. In fact, he wished that obligation had not bound him to the bell, at least not so tightly, so intimately. Of course, he rang it during emergencies, such as the case at hand, but it also rang, whether he wanted it to or not, when he turned a corner too quickly, or got up from his seat too abruptly. It became a real problem when he slept; the slightest tossing and turning and he'd be rudely awakened by it. Of course, whenever he stepped up to use the urinal, the situation was embarrassing at best.

"The wind and the waves," the steward gasped, helping the first officer push the pole, "they're not letting us get close enough to him! This is hardly a successful rescue attempt, and it's unlikely that we'll get those promotions you mentioned!"

"I know," the first officer nodded, clenching his teeth, his hands more than full, "it's hard to get ahead in this career."

From the other side of the deck, a handful of sailors looked on, sweeping up the ashes of their fellow crewmen, pausing periodically to watch the rescue. The wind made their attempts futile, and guaranteed all the deceased a burial at sea. The wind continued to wreak the same havoc on the slipshod rescue attempt, when it suddenly turned things to the rescuer's favour.

Christopher, by now frantic in his helpless state, was raised up by a wave that carried him directly towards the net. He panicked. How could he grab hold of it? What was he to do? They should be using a gaff hook for him. Yes, that was it! He was about to cry out when he experienced the oddest sensation. The net, much to his surprise, as small as it was, had closed in and around him. In fact, it seemed to pass right *through him*. Before he could examine what he felt, he was being raised up out of the water. The mesh pressed in on his nose, almost forcing his lips shut, as he let out a muffled cry. He felt abnormally light, almost dizzy. He was being pulled up much too quickly. Something was very wrong. His senses reeled. He was aware of everything that was happening, as unbelievable as it was, yet he was powerless to do anything about it.

"Careful," the first officer shouted to the steward, as they turned the pole to the right, bringing Christopher up over the railing.

"What the hell?" Christopher gasped, dripping wet, dangling high above the deck, twisting in the wind, dizzy, the mesh pressing in around him. "What the hell? What's going on! I intend to complain to the Captain! I was better off bobbing around in the water!"

"He's ranting!" the steward blurted, straining to help the first mate direct the pole.

"Get me down from here!" Christopher cried.

"He does seem quite beside himself," the first officer nodded, as they swung Christopher down towards the deck. "Set him down easy."

The steward, lacking experience in such matters, served only to frustrate the first officer's rescue attempts. The wind blew up suddenly, catching them both off guard. Christopher swung against a cargo hatch. He let out a terrible cry, and then fell unconscious. Dropping the pole, the first officer gave the steward a critical look. The steward shrugged his shoulders and tried to look away.

"Well, I suppose that'll calm him," the first officer removed his hat, wiping his brow with his sleeve.

The steward, hands on hips, looked down at Christopher, or what was there of him.

"Well," he sighed, "what do we do now?"

"I'm not sure," the first officer knelt over Christopher, "this is beyond the scope of my duties. I suppose we'll have to take ... *this* to the Captain and see what he says."

The steward stepped back. The sailors, still busy on the other side of the deck, stopped with their sweeping. Looking towards the first officer, they *thought* they heard him clearly, but hoped they were mistaken. They were ready to race off the deck, if they had to. The mere mention of *him* set it off. Yes, the Captain would know of this matter; he'd have to be involved. He wasn't the Captain for nothing. He had achieved his rank through heritage; his father was a sailor off the coast of Africa. He had achieved his rank through determination and perseverance; he had fought valiantly aboard many a war ship. He had achieved unlimited knowledge and wisdom from countless years spent upon all the seas spanning the globe. But most off all, he achieved his rank because of that third eye in the middle of his forehead that focused mental energy into a destructive ray that could destroy small vessels and set oceans ablaze. Yes, in the end, he had achieved his rank through fear.

"Do you really think that's necessary?" the steward trembled, for it was cold, the wind becoming quite fierce.

"Yes," the first officer nodded, trying to keep his bell from ringing in the wind, and in front of the other sailors, "We have to see the Captain. Grab hold of ..." he paused, looking down at Christopher, "*him* before that storm comes up and washes us overboard!"

They plodded up stairs, down walkways, wind and waves shooting spray, making their footing dangerous. The steward, unable to keep his balance at times, and afraid of what was ahead, held Christopher tightly by the hair, cradling him under his left arm, trying not to drop him. The first officer kept stopping to prevent his bell from ringing, much to his embarrassment. They were soon at the control room, the lights penetrating out through water splashed glass and ocean spray. The steward allowed the first officer to go first, out of fear and custom. Thrusting the door open, the wind roaring up behind them, they came upon the Captain.

The Captain was slumped against the steering wheel, a half-empty bottle of vodka in his right hand, barely keeping himself off the ground.

"Oh, lucky for us," the first officer turned to the steward, shivering behind him, "he's got himself drunk again. He'll be easier to deal with."

"What's going on?" Christopher suddenly cried, almost causing the steward to drop him. "Where am I?"

The first officer ran in and helped the Captain up as best he could, propping him against the wheel.

"The Captain will see you now," he turned to Christopher, as if to answer his question.

The steward, however, was reluctant to bring Christopher in. He stood at the door, mouth ajar, shivering, the wind roaring behind him. He had heard many questionable stories about the Captain, but never met him face to face. And now he knew that all those stories were true, not just bizarre concoctions of drunken sailors gone mad from too many weeks at sea. It was almost too much for him to comprehend. Seeing the Captain's weathered face and that great unknown - the eye of the soul, the key to forgotten and mysterious corners of the mind, there in full view, both terrible and fascinating - he almost forgot he had a man's head beneath his arm. What mysteries float in the Captain's head? Mystery, the unknown, breeds fear. Everything in the Captain's mind - the rage, the guilt of years spent at sea, pent-up emotions - could explode at any moment, bursting out through that third eye.

"Give that to me," the first officer leaned towards him, taking Christopher by the hair, pulling him in and slamming the door so the steward and the upcoming storm were locked out.

"Watch what you're doing!" Christopher cried, as the first officer plunked him down on a table. "I intend to complain about the service and the conditions aboard this ship! Although I'm not sure what those conditions were previously, I sense that they've deteriorated somewhat."

"What do we have here?" the Captain stuttered, looking at Christopher and then the first officer.

Facing the Captain now, Christopher was speechless. Considering everything he'd been through, the flurry of bizarre emotions, fears and thoughts, this was but another rung in the ladder, heading straight up to insanity.

"I know why you're looking at me like that," the Captain belched, "because I'm drunk!"

"I found him overboard, sir," the first officer saluted. "I happened to be on the aft deck, ringing the bell to signal the approaching storm, as you ordered, when I heard his cries. He was bobbing in the waves. I called to the steward for help, and we proceeded to rescue him."

"What were you doing overboard?" the Captain growled, trying to stand up straight. "Don't you know there are rules aboard this vessel?"

"This is ridiculous," Christopher began, trying to shake his head. "Look at me! Something terrible has happened and I want to know who's responsible. How can I be blamed for being overboard? Can't you see that, or are you so drunk that you're limited to simply steering the ship? The most important question is how did this happen and, what's foremost in the back of my mind - where's my body?"

"You've picked a late hour to make such requests," the Captain stumbled forward, almost dropping his bottle, "and, on top of it all, we're heading into a storm. Can't you come back tomorrow morning when everything's blown over? I'm liable to be sober then."

"I can't believe what I'm hearing," Christopher shot an angry glance at the Captain and then the first officer, who was still at attention, but ready to catch the Captain if he should fall. "It just isn't convenient or practical for me to return tomorrow. Several questions have to be answered. You don't understand what I've just been through! First, lost at sea - powerless, immobile, helpless, without a clue, my life washing up, floating around me. And now this shocking revelation," he paused, looking down at the table he was resting on - "the reason for my paralyses, my helplessness. How can you just blow this off as a common event that can be dealt with tomorrow morning? Don't you see that something isn't right here? Doesn't the sight of me and my strange plight shock you?"

"Shock me?" the Captain roared, the first officer stepped away instinctively, closing his eyes briefly. "Look at *me*," he stabbed a finger towards the centre of his forehead. "Do I look normal to you? Do you have any idea what I've been through? You've just had a rough evening, but I've lived with *this* my entire life. Do you know what it's like to live with something like this, something so powerful it's terrible - a burden, not a blessing? My family had to move me from school to school and town to town as my playmates went missing and house after house burnt down. And now, do you think I'm happy as a Captain aboard a ship, in such close confines with other men? Hold on a second," he ran over to the wheel, turned it a little, and then returned. "There's a very strong head wind tonight. Right then, as I was saying, I've lost almost all of my crew since the start of this cruise. Every time I turn around I invite disaster! There's always something ablaze, or a hole in the hull. It's my father's fault, of course; he got me hooked on sailing. And I know what you're thinking," he wagged a finger at Christopher, who was speechless, having got a better look at the Captain. "You're thinking: why not end it? Well, do you know how many times I've tried to plunge a knife into this chest?" he ripped open his uniform, spilling some vodka. "Once or twice, but I usually have a couple of drinks and then forget about it."

The Captain walked over to a chair and sat down across from Christopher.

"I like being out at sea," he crossed his legs, "the air does me good."

"I'm sorry," Christopher began, "I didn't mean to diminish the significance of your suffering, but I really must press my case. I suppose that, in a way, you know how I feel right now and, hopefully, you can sympathize with me and help me get to the bottom of this. I'm not asking for much, just some help for a helpless man. After some careful thought and recollection, difficult in my state of mind - and not that I wasn't paying attention to your story - I've managed to put a few pieces of the puzzle together. Now I think I know how you can help me solve this problem once and for all." Christopher paused, partly for dramatic effect, partly out of a strange feeling of reluctance. "Could you please summon my wife? I'm almost certain that I saw her peering out a porthole. Well, I'm certain she's my wife - who else could it have been? *At least she knew me -* she cried down to me! Regardless, it makes sense to find her. Maybe then we can find out what happened, locate my body, and get this nonsense over with!"

"That sounds like the best course of action," the Captain nodded, sipping his vodka, "first officer, ring for his wife."

"My pleasure," the officer saluted.

Christopher rolled his eyes. He hated that ringing. He had to look away from the first officer, pulling his bell-rope in front of him. He wished he could summon his wife himself.

"You rang?" Clea appeared at the door in her housecoat, half concealed, the wind roaring in.

"Yes," the first officer took a deep breath, collecting himself, shocked at her sudden arrival, "we have your husband's head."

"Oh," Clea stepped in, closing the door behind her, "I thought that was it bobbing around out there. How fortunate you found it, with the storm getting so bad."

The first officer, lighting a cigarette, just nodded.

"Clea," Christopher burst, "Look at me. What's happened to me? What's going on?"

"Well my dear," Clea leaned over him, pulling her housecoat tighter, "you were leaning over the bow, perhaps admiring something in the waves, maybe out of lack of anything better to do, and your head simply came loose and fell straight down into the water."

"That can't be," Christopher cried. "Look at me - that's no explanation! I must have been struck from behind. Foul play is at work!"

"But I was there, behind you," Clea insisted. "I saw it happen."

"I don't believe it," Christopher looked towards the first officer, still enjoying a cigarette, and the Captain, snoozing in his chair. "Something is very wrong here. I have to know why this has happened to me."

"I don't know why he's so excited," the first officer shrugged, looking towards Clea. "It seems a likely story."

"He's always been headstrong," Clea crossed her arms.

"If your story is true," Christopher burst, "if it really happened as you said, then why didn't you immediately sound the alarm? Do you know what it was like for me out there? I can hardly describe it, the emptiness I felt. If my head just rolled right off my shoulders in front of you, then why didn't you do something - anything?"

"It was the most spontaneous thing you ever did," Clea replied, "and it soon became a real adventure for me. I was taken in by it all, I admit. I had to really wrestle with you - you're body that is; it was difficult to get it to cooperate, running all over, into this and that, scaring the crew. But at the same time, you were full of a certain playfulness that appealed to me. It wasn't like before; the change was instantaneous, I guess. No more worries. No more lamenting. Of course, I had to mother you a bit more, stop you from wandering into other people's rooms, or sticking your hand into the toilet, but it was still a welcome change."

Suddenly, the Captain awoke. When a storm was brewing, he became full of a certain urgency that prevented him from getting too calm or comfortable in any given situation. As a result, he was forever in a state of subdued readiness, always anticipating disaster. He ran over and tried the radio. Nothing but static. He adjusted the various knobs and dials, but to no avail. He turned the radio off.

"Ah, that thing's never worked," he waved his hand, returning to his seat, falling back to sleep.

"Clea," Christopher spoke softly, wanting her to come closer, "we have to get off this ship. We can sort out what's happened to me later. But now, let's just find my body and leave before we end up going down with this wreck!"

"That won't be so easy," she sat next to him. "I haven't been able to find your body since dinner. I fear it's lost, or gone overboard."

"Actually, come to think of it," The first officer spoke up, butting his cigarette into an ashtray, "I saw a headless body on the aft deck, throwing some papers overboard, about an hour ago."

"You have to take me there," Christopher pleaded.

"I don't know," Clea sighed.

"What do you mean?" Christopher looked up at her, astonished. "We have to get off this ship before it goes down!"

"You're boring me already with your worries," she turned her back to him. "I'd rather *really live*, if only for a moment, and go down quickly than live forever with your tediousness!"

"Clea," Christopher frowned, wishing the first officer wasn't there, listening to everything. Christopher felt violated by his presence. Perhaps the first officer sensed this, excusing himself to use the washroom. Christopher waited, listening for the washroom door locking; when the ringing began, he started up again, confident that the first officer was indisposed.

"Clea, whatever do you mean?"

"I'm sick and tired of your worries getting between us. Now you've went and pulled this stunt, and somehow you find me to blame. You suggest that I'm not telling the truth, as if the world is out to get you and I'm merely an accomplice. Well, you should take this entire thing as a sign of your severe self-indulgence. You always take your meagre problems and blow them out of proportion, as if your trials and tribulations are all that matter. In the process, you suck the life out of everything! There's nothing of interest between us because there's nothing there for *me*. There's just no fun anymore."

"I didn't know that things were getting that bad," Christopher looked up at Clea, humbled by what he heard. "You should have told me long ago. I guess I didn't have my head on straight. How can I apologise? I know I take work too seriously, but I'm only concerned about the future - *our* future. Perhaps you're right, I should concentrate more on the present and live for the moment. I guess I let my worries overtake me, and in the process I've neglected the one I love, taken you for granted."

"Yes," Clea sighed, "something like that."

"What's that compass say?" The first officer cried suddenly, exiting the washroom.

He ran over to the compass and nervously checked the other instruments.

"I thought a change was coming over," he thought aloud.

"What's wrong now?" Christopher asked.

"We're way off course," the first officer shook his head. "We're no longer out at sea!"

"What do you mean?" Christopher panicked, Clea moving closer to him. "Where are we then?"

The first officer removed his hat, quickly running his fingers through his hair, giving the distinct impression that a mistake had been made; he wasn't very good at hiding it. He rubbed his forehead, perhaps intentionally avoiding the question, perhaps wishing he hadn't raised concern. Pulling his hat back on, he paused, then looked Christopher directly in the eye.

"We're in the headwaters."

"Is that bad?" Christopher immediately asked, Clea sitting next to him, her hand on his head, comforting him as best she could, given the circumstances.

"Well, it's not what I expected," the first officer rubbed his chin, looking over the controls. "This vessel isn't built to handle it. It's uncharted territory, probably too shallow. But with the Captain's stubborn will, and my aggressive tenacity, we'll plough through."

"Don't think I haven't heard a word that's been said," the Captain suddenly awoke; "I'm a restless sleeper who only keeps himself intoxicated to avoid harming my crew. Now, what's this about the headwaters?"

"We're way off course," the first officer took the wheel.

"I see," the Captain stretched, rising slowly from his chair, "and with the storm brewing we're being sent headlong into disaster!"

"What can we do?" Clea cried.

"Sorry if I alarmed you two," the Captain took a gulp of vodka. "It's just your standard uncharted course, like a drama that has yet to be acted out. We have to play our roles and hope for the best. The parts, of course, are mapped out for us, almost predetermined; it's our actions that lead us astray. Anyway, I'm the world-worn, aging sea Captain, with an eye for wisdom, power, and stubborn pride. My first officer is the ambitious up-and-coming youth. Anxious to learn from me, to follow in my footsteps. Full of a certain life - a boyish optimism that I lost long ago to pessimism, bitterness, and half a bottle of Scotch. One day he'll be the ringmaster," he paused to pat the first officer, smiling shyly. "And your wife, she's pretty much caught up in it. Victimized by circumstance, in her housecoat, she's the classic heroine. And you ..." the Captain roared, outstretching a hand towards Christopher, as the ship rolled violently, "well, it goes without saying - you're the headliner!"

"So, we should just sit tight and pray for the best?" Christopher ventured.

"Yeah," the Captain sighed, "we can try that too."

"Look down at the forward deck!" the first officer called out.

They raced to the windows, Clea leaving Christopher behind on the table, the Captain almost stumbling. They strained to see through the wind, rain, and ocean spray. But judging by the looks they exchanged, they all saw it. There was Christopher's other half, running wildly about, throwing papers into the wind, blind to the storm around him, whipped by wind and water, nearly washed away, pausing only to straighten his tie.

"What is it?" Christopher called over, unable to bare the suspense. "What's going on?"

"It's your body!" Clea cried, racing over and touching his cheek, unable to embrace him. "It really was on the forward deck! If only you could see it, flailing about madly; it's so unlike you. It's refreshing - even exciting!"

The Captain, being the best versed for an emergency like this, immediately formed a plan of action.

"Clea, Christopher," he called their names, without ever being introduced, he was that wise, his third eye blinking every so often, although it usually kept closed when he drank, "you can trust me, as your Captain and a friend. Yes, it's strange, but I consider you two my friends. Believe me when I tell you I've been to sea for many years and my boat is full of seamen. My first officer will attest to that, because with all his accomplishments aboard this vessel, he's a ringer for me when I was young!"

"It's probably true," the first officer turned to them, and then back to the wheel.

"Anyway," the Captain continued, "to make a long story short, which is something I like to do when I'm drunk and lacking attention to detail, the situation is like this: the conditions out on that deck are terrible, with gale force winds, waves breaking over the railing, and poor visibility - a highly dangerous situation! So, Clea - since you've only got your housecoat on, I recommend strongly, as the Captain of this vessel, with several years experience at sea, that you wear a hat when you take Christopher out there to get his body back."

"But how will we find our way back?" Clea asked, as the Captain handed her Christopher's head, pushing her out the door.

"I don't think this is the best laid plan," Christopher expressed his concern, almost drowned out by the wind and rain.

"Don't worry," the Captain patted him on the head, "my first officer will climb up to the crow's nest and ring his bell."

"I will?" the first officer paused with his steering.

"Yes," the Captain continued, "ring your bell so they can find their way back."

The eye of the storm was upon them now, unwinding its rage, a mysterious but destructive force. Any man with a shred of common sense became filled with fear. Wind and rain pelted down on the control room windows. The ship, rocking back and forth, was plunging through the headwaters to an uncertain destination.

"I don't know about this," the first officer shook his head.

"What?" the Captain hollered, the wind and rain roaring in through the door. "What's the matter now?"

The first officer was silent, his face reddened. He looked down, unable to face the Captain.

"Well, out with it!" the Captain hollered. "We don't have all night!"

"Ringing my bell *again*, in front of that woman?" the first officer burst, shaking his head. "It doesn't seem right. I'm embarrassed. It was alright at first, she caught me off guard with her quick appearance, but now she might take it the wrong way. Everything's so serious now."

"Oh come on now," the Captain rolled his eyes, "you're always ringing that thing when it's not really needed - at night, to some passing ship, knowing full well that you won't be seen. Or, even worse, you ring it without thinking or caring. This vessel depends on a good ringer. Now's your chance to truly prove yourself! Now get up there, ring that bell, with purpose and intent, and be proud - be a man! And take a raincoat."

"I never gave you *this* much trouble!" Christopher cried above the roaring wind and crashing waves, tucked securely under Clea's arm. "You call this fun?"

"Not at the moment," she nearly fell over, caught by the wind and the slippery deck; "like anything, you have your ups and downs."

The body was elusive at best. Perhaps it sensed its approaching return to imprisonment, having been free for so long. Perhaps it somehow sensed the ringing, with the first officer now perched carefully atop the control room, and knew that something was up. Christopher hated the ringing almost as much as the sight of himself running wild, without control. But he longed for a union, to be one again. It was strange, watching his body run free. He gained a new perspective, to say the least. He was in a unique position to do so. He was able to think about things carefully, at least as carefully as possible, considering he was tucked beneath Clea's arm, dripping wet. He was able to watch Clea interact with his body, lashing out with her free arm, trying to grasp the soaking wet business suit that was a favourite of his. It was as though he was watching a bizarre home video, except this was much more immediate, more frantic, but not without its moments of humour and compassion. The body played with her hair, toyed with her housecoat. She laughed, even in the gale-force winds, water splashing everywhere. She had to drag it along like a child, sometimes cooperating, but usually not.

Everything seemed new to the body and, needless to say,

there was no such thing as social grace or etiquette. The body had few reservations about anything. It would disappear briefly, pulling away from Clea during a flash of lightning and a splash of waves across the deck. They called out to it, forgetting that it could not hear. But then, as suddenly as it disappeared, it would reappear in a potato sack, hopping along, racing past them to the stairs. Such shenanigans were really wearing thin, even at that early stage.

Despite it all, they continued to press on towards the ringing, and the stairs leading up to the control room. The body was skipping one minute and caressing Clea the next. Christopher had to call off any potential moments of sudden, unexpected passion, reminding Clea of their urgency. He was surprised his body had managed to function this long without him. He was racked with questions. How his body kept the tie on he'll never know. His body was too preoccupied with the tie, trying desperately to straighten it amidst the wind and rain, slowing their progress considerably. Christopher silently swore an oath to wear a turtleneck on their next cruise. Looking away from his body, surveying the area as best he could from beneath Clea's arm, he saw his notes and money all over the deck, soaking wet, washing away. Flashes of lightening illuminated it all. Of course, Christopher's body was still very much aloof with regards to his thoughts and concerns, let alone the situation they were in.

Through some effort, they found themselves forcing their way up the stairs, the ringing reaching an apex now as they approached. The door to the control room flung open and in they leaped, followed by fierce winds and a splash of water. They were soaked to the skin. The Captain was absorbed with his radio. Adjusting the various knobs and dials, it hummed and hissed, yet refused all incoming transmissions and stopped any from being sent. His patience was getting the best of him. The young couple looked on behind him, hoping to get a message through, hoping to be saved. The Captain shook his head fiercely, his eye glowing with anger, the radio hissing and humming. He brought his fist down on the radio, then tried to calm himself before things got serious.

"You see," he looked towards the couple, taking his seat, breathing deeply, pointing towards the radio, "this has been the bulk of the problem all along!"

"Can it be repaired?" Clea asked, shivering. "Let Christopher look at it; he used to be good with things like that."

The Captain looked over at Christopher, still cradled in Clea's arm. His body ... well, she had to stand on it to stop it from running wild in the control room.

"I'm willing to give it a try," Christopher spoke up, winking at the Captain.

The door flung open once again and the first officer stumbled in, soaking wet, shivering, but with a big smile across his face. He felt tremendously accomplished and adequate. He had never rang for so long before. The fact he was nervous - with the storm upon them and so much responsibility placed on his shoulders, or around his waist - did not prevent him from carrying out his duty to the best of his ability. And he had been a success!

"Excellent work," the Captain commended him. The first officer nodded shyly, lighting a cigarette, "but there's no time for patting everyone on the back. There's a crisis at hand. Obviously, we have to solve this problem before we can make any headway. "

The Captain looked over to Christopher, still cradled in Clea's arms. She was wiping his brow, which made it difficult to pay close attention to the Captain.

"I think you know what this means, Christopher," the Captain said.

"Yes," Christopher answered, pausing to think everything over, hoping to be honest without being embarrassed "I've been too long without. It's hard for me to describe what I've been through, how I felt, but it was so jarring, so eye opening, that it left a profound impression on me. I realise now that I must keep a careful balance between mind and body," at this point, he looked up to Clea, who was smiling, "because if one becomes separated from the other, chaos erupts." Christopher paused. The Captain, listening intently, nodded approvingly. The first officer puffed away in the corner, arms crossed, trying to keep warm. Clea gently caressed Christopher's forehead. "I don't know what else to say," he looked up at her, continuing. "I've been through enough. I've felt complete emptiness, within myself and between you and me. We were drifting apart without even knowing it. It took some unusual circumstances to get us to realize our folly, or *my* folly, but now I'm ready. I've learnt my lesson - the hard way! I want to be complete again. I feel as if things will be much better this time. I'm sorry I lost my head."

"It's funny," Clea smiled, "but everything you and I have been through - it was worth it. I'm glad you're back, and having seen a different side of you, I know there is hope for us."

"Captain," Christopher called over to him, feeling very accomplished, "let's get that radio fixed and get things underway!"

"What do you mean?" the Captain sprang forward in his chair, his eyes wide, sweat rolling down his brow. Seeing the young couple giving him odd looks, he stared briefly into space, shook his head, and got up. He stretched, twisting back and forth, and then swung his arms around. Stopping, he took a deep breath. "I had a bad dream just now," he said.

The Captain was always a man to rush to duty. He could identify a situation that needed his assistance and put a plan in motion immediately, even if he just woke up - from bad dreams, no less. While the Captain and the first officer restrained Christopher's body, Clea put his head back on. It took her some time, a little twisting and turning, but she soon had it on straight. She stepped away, as did the Captain and the first officer. Christopher, now together, complete, quivered slightly. He winced, his shoulders shrugging. It took him awhile to get back to the old routine. His feet flopped around a bit, his arms flung out uncontrollably, but he was basically fully functional. His first gesture was to take Clea into his arms, hugging her tightly. Then he immediately set about fixing his tie.

"Well," the Captain slapped him on the shoulder, "now that were all together, how about trying to fix the radio?"

While Clea, the Captain, and the first officer watched the storm rage around the ship, Christopher set to work. In the past, he was well acquainted with electronics and gadgetry, but now he was a bit rusty; he hoped his memory would not fail him. Soon, the static bursts and deep, almost guttural, humming took the form of voices, ever so faint. The lightning caused break-ups, but it was obvious he was having some success.

"Mayday, mayday," Christopher attempted transmission, adjusting various knobs and dials, a high pitched whine filling the control room. "I think I've repaired it enough to send a message through," he called to the others.

"Let me try," the Captain raced over, grabbing the receiver from him. "I'm keen on these sorts of things. I'm the Captain!"

With his ear pressed against the radio, the Captain made his plea for help. Throughout the static, humming, and moments of dead air, a voice could be heard. The Captain nodded, as the voice continued.

"The storm is coming to an end!" he turned to Christopher and Clea, holding each other tightly. The first officer breathed a sigh of relief. He'd had more than enough bell ringing to do him for the rest of the week.

"Wait!" the Captain pressed his ear back against the radio. "We're approaching a harbour!"

"Everything will be alright now," Christopher kissed Clea.

"The way is clear for us," the Captain motioned for the first officer to come closer. "Type in these coordinates. Check the compass and set the wheel."

"Aye, aye, Captain," the officer saluted, running to the controls.

"The storm is clearing faster than expected!" the Captain continued to listen to the reports. "Wave action is dying down, the moon is shining through, visibility is excellent, and the harbour is very close now. It's almost too good to be true!"

Christopher and Clea were overjoyed, almost dancing, caught up in the warmth of their tight embrace.

"But wait, that's not all!" the Captain cried, waving his hand at the couple. "Did one of you enter a lottery?"

"Yes," Clea cried, grabbing Christopher's collar, jumping up and down, "yes, yes I bought us a ticket before we left! I can't believe this! I can't believe this is happening to us!"

"Well you didn't win," the Captain shook his head, "but we'll get home safely."

******

Out on the forward deck, Christopher revelled in the moonlight. The storm had long since passed. The harbour lights were visible, on the horizon, straight ahead. He leaned over the railing, scanning the waves, alive with eels, breaking alongside the ocean liner. The sea was so alive with eels that its surface boiled with activity for as far as the eye could see. They seemed to be the sole cause of all wave action, the wind having died down to almost nil.

Every once and awhile, staring down at the water, he'd get a chill, like electricity flowing up his spine, performing acupuncture on his neck. Rubbing his neck, he stepped away from the railing, fearing another bout of decapitation. He learnt his lesson the first time; he was a quick study. Two arms wrapped around his waist from behind, startling him, but there quickly followed a familiar sense of comfort.

"Letting curiosity get the best of you?" Clea kissed the back of his neck, having just returned from getting changed.

"I suppose," He smiled, letting her sway him back and forth, "I've always been fascinated by the sea."

"Oh look," Clea released him, stepping up to the railing, watching the eels boil up and splash across the water's surface in the moonlight, "isn't it lovely. So romantic!"

The couple paced slowly around the front deck, hand in hand, admiring the stars overhead, encountering the odd overzealous eel that had somehow ended up on the deck, knocking it overboard. Only the gentle sound of the ship's engines and the splash of eels far below accompanied them.

Soon the ship was sliding into port, surrounded by eels. The harbour was alive with them! An eerie mist coated everything in the harbour, cancelling out the moon and the stars. The first officer, sensing his duty, climbed on top of the control room and began to ring his bell, warning other vessels in the harbour; visibility had become that bad. From high atop the deck, however, Christopher and Clea could make out a long line-up of sailors, no doubt waiting to board; the Captain's new crew.

"Here we are," the Captain came up behind and squeezed their shoulders. But he did not startle them; they could smell the vodka approaching. "Safe and sound - a true success!"

"We appreciate everything you've done for us," Clea shook his hand. "You really helped us to see through it all."

"Make no mention of it," the Captain waved his hand, shaking his head, laughing, "it's all part of my job. Besides, Christopher did most of the work. It was just up to me, and my first officer, of course, to help him along. Of course," he gave her hand a friendly squeeze, "it wouldn't have been possible at all without you. If you weren't there for Christopher, in his time of need and self-doubt, then we all would have gone down with the ship! But now," the Captain became quite serious, "let's get you two home, where you belong."

Down on the dock, finally on terra firma, Christopher and Clea were greatly relieved. Of course, the cruise had been a worthwhile experience for them both. They had learnt so much, but they were too exhausted to attach any more significance to it; they just wanted to get home and rest.

They followed the Captain along, as he inspected his new crew. They had no choice; it was too foggy to venture out on their own. The first officer sat atop the Captain's shoulders, ringing his bell, warning people they were coming through. The sight thrilled all the sailors, gathered on the dock. They looked upon the Captain, with his first officer atop his shoulders, bell ringing, the third eye gleaming, and they knew that adventure was in store. The line-up of sailors seemed endless. It seemed like the inspection would never end!

"My new seamen!" the Captain raised his arm, smiling proudly, his first officer almost falling from his shoulders. "Soon my vessel will be full again!"

They finally veered away from the never-ending line-up. Christopher and Clea had no idea where they were being led, but they trusted the Captain and his first officer implicitly. Surprisingly, they were not alone in the fog. Several other young couples floated in and out of view, in various states of dress and undress, some clad in nightgowns, housecoats, and pyjamas. Several of them approached the Captain, asking when the next departure time was. But the Captain, determined to lead Christopher and Clea home, exhausted from having his first officer atop his shoulders, and still somewhat drunk, hardly had the patience to answer their questions.

"Tickets are available down at the dock," was all he'd say, waving his hands, pressing on, his third eye gleaming.

"Was it worth it?" a young woman grabbed Clea by the arm, clutching her husband's head in her right hand. He seemed quite embarrassed by it all.

"Yes," Clea held Christopher closer, "yes, it was."

The Captain urged them on. The gateway was in front of them, and the path leading up to their house. Home at last.

"Here we are," Christopher smiled. "I don't know how to thank you - *we* don't know how to thank you."

"Once again," the Captain waved his hand, "it was my duty,

and it wouldn't have been possible without the two of you, working together. But I really must be going; my shoulders ache terribly and I need aspirin. Got a new crew as well, waiting for me. My work never ends."

"Thank you, once again," Clea shook his hand, reaching up to shake the first officer's hand as well.

"You're welcome," the Captain smiled shyly. "I'm sure you'll enjoy a bright future together; he has a good head on his shoulders."

Christopher and Clea, standing at their gate, waved goodbye to the Captain and his first officer. The first officer, turned right around on the Captain's shoulders, waved and waved until they disappeared into the fog. Only the ringing could be heard, and even that was fading as they headed back to the harbour.

Inside the house, preparing for bed, Christopher and Clea were almost too tired to utter another word. In fact, Christopher had dozed off in his suit and tie! Clea lay next to him, watching him breath softly. She gently caressed her stomach. She decided to tell him the good news in the morning.

"It" – Monster from the Unknown

"It" sat in the chair, motionless. "It" wasn't thinking about anything in particular. "It" rarely did. "It" was content. Suddenly, the telephone rang.

'That must be the United States!' "It" thought excitedly.

Under close observation, one might notice "It" moving, ever so slightly, as the telephone rang on. Yes, "It" *stirred*, almost causing the chair to rock, ever so slightly. But "It" restricted movement. Why bother expending energy? In fact, why be excited? A call from the States could only mean one thing: "It" would have to *do something*.

Luckily, the assistant picked up the telephone before "It" became too flustered. "It" wasn't accustomed to so much activity within the office, at least not all at once.

'It's the President of the United States,' the assistant called over to "It", cupping his hand over the receiver. 'Should I tell him you're in?'

"It" quivered ever so slightly, like "It" usually did when the President called. The assistant, highly trained and accustomed to such matters, took this as a yes. He brought the telephone over to "It". Not knowing quite where to hold the telephone (he never did) he simply held it as close to "It" as possible. You see, "It" had no ears. The assistant could hear the President on the other end of the line hollering to be heard. The President knew full well that "It" was hard of hearing, having dealt with "It" many times in the past, yet he was also fully aware that "It" was highly cooperative and seldom argumentative.

As things turned out, the President had called regarding matters pertaining to the Free Trade Agreement. The President needed "It's" permission to build several thousand American owned and operated department stores in Canada, all selling clothing made exclusively by peasant laborers in Mexico. In return, thousands of minimum wage part-time jobs would be created for Canadian citizens - something for everyone to cheer about.

"It" agreed immediately, quivering all over. The resulting

part-time jobs would be greatly appreciated by those hit hardest by recent cut-backs - including the poor, the homeless, the unemployed, the working class, the middle class, students, recent graduates, doctors, nurses, teachers, farmers, fisherman, and anyone else living in Canada. Of course, the Mexicans stood to gain as well; since none of them could afford the clothes they made, they might as well sell them in Canada and let the Americans profit.

At this point, although it's hard to believe, "It" almost fell off the chair. This often happened when "It" got too enthusiastic. Being a good diplomat, "It" usually kept extreme displays of emotion at bay. Of course, "It" never spoke either, for lack of a mouth. This added to the effect, making "It" a very popular diplomat indeed. But don't think this means the assistant had to relay "It's" response to the President. The President hung up shortly after stating his intentions, confident that "It" would go along with his plan, and not wishing to waste time listening to silence - or "It's" assistant, for that matter.

By now, "It" was exhausted. Although "It" had no eyes (how could "It" be expected to have eyes?) "It" sensed the assistant moving towards the door. Was it time for him to leave? "It" didn't know. "It" had no concept of time. Even if there was a clock on the wall, and there very well could have been, "It" was too dim-witted to figure out how to use something like that.

As it turned out, the assistant was not leaving after all. Instead, "It" sensed yet another person in the room. But "It" couldn't be sure. "It's" senses, if they could be called senses at all, were somewhat distracted by what "It" detected, rightly or wrongly, as a subtle change in the climate within the office. Chances are it was just an air-conditioner kicking in, thus exciting "It's" primitive nervous system, if it could be called a nervous system at all.

And now the problems arose, which were not uncommon at this high level of government. The assistant (who "It" finally learned to recognize just last week, by the way) had to convince "It" that a visitor had arrived. "It" had to be convinced beyond the shadow of a doubt, before allowing the assistant to sign anything or order Parliament to take action, if action was needed. As a result, a battery of tests was implemented, taking several hours.

The assistant, by now accustomed to the process, used every trick in the book including: electrical shock, rigorous rubbing, screaming and yelling, flicking the lights on and off, stomping up and down, and finally a failed attempt at normal conversation. These combined tactics worked wonders. In less than three hours - a new record - "It" realised that the visitor was Mr. Morningfeather. In a matter of nanoseconds (not that "It" would understand what they were) "It" computed Mr. Morningfeather's politically correct name, which was The Young North American Indian Environmentalist Fellow. Yes, that was "It's" strong point - coming up with catchy phrases and titles to amaze colleagues and thrill reporters.

"It" had few memories. Most became lost when "It" had to ingest breakfast through the slow, painful process of osmosis. Yet, "It" strained - if you could call it straining (no, in fact, "It" quivered) - and recalled that the Young North American Indian Environmentalist Fellow was the Minister of Young North American Indian Environmentalist Fellow Affairs. "It" had granted him the position after he wrote an agreeable article in a multi-cultural magazine, a magazine that was funded, produced, published, and written by the government, except for the article in question, which The Young North American Indian Environmentalist Fellow was allowed to sign his name to.

Yes, "It" was proud, or maybe just content (it was always hard to tell). And "It" was never as proud as when the press came flooding into the office. This was the only time "It" got up - or even moved. The general feeling of approaching press, even from several metres away, caused "It" to rise to the occasion. Pure instinct - that's why "It" was in charge! And the cameramen went wild, seeing "It" posing next to the Young North American Indian Environmentalist Fellow.

This would make "It" popular with all sorts of people. And why not? After all, "It" gave The Young North American Indian Environmentalist Fellow his seat in the House of Commons, which was near the back, in the corner. Actually, there wasn't a seat there at all – it was a stool from the cafeteria. And when the House of Commons got busy, which it always did, space was limited, so The Young North American Indian Environmentalist Fellow had to sit outside in the hallway. But he could get into the House of

Commons when things had ended and everyone filed out. Then he might sit and relax for awhile in the silence, contemplating his situation, perhaps thinking up new legislation to better the lives of his people and end discrimination of all types. This sort of thing was permitted, but not encouraged. The janitor would ask The Young North American Indian Environmentalist Fellow to return to his office. And when he said *his office* he meant the janitor's office, because they had to share.

Perhaps more importantly, and on an optimistic note, all the other ministers spoke highly of The Young North American Indian Environmentalist Fellow, if they spoke of him at all. Most of them commented favourably on the fact that he was always on time, as they raced past him - seated in the hallway, trying to get in before the doors locked. Of course, none of this had to reach the press.

The Young North American Indian Environmentalist Fellow's moment in the sun quickly ended. The assistant cleared the press out. "It" returned to the chair. The photo op with "It" was over. Back to business as usual. The Young North American Indian Environmentalist Fellow, figuring incorrectly that he'd been called upon to perform some function, decided to air his grievances. The list was a mile long. But before he could get a word out, he was knocked down from behind.

Mr. Pockets walked over him, annoyed with anything standing in his way. Mr. Pockets could see "It" whenever he wanted to - without question. No press, or Young North American Indian Environmentalist-type fellows, could take priority over him. "It", quivering all over, was obviously glad to see Mr. Pockets. Of course, "It" had a politically correct term for Mr. Pockets as well, one which was developed eons ago, one which "It's" semblance of a memory allowed "It" to recall. Mr. Pocket's politically correct title was: White Corporate Fellow with Heavy Briefcase, Alcoholic Wife, Three Kids, and No Intentions of Giving it Up. Well, as it turned out, White Corporate Fellow with Heavy Briefcase, Alcoholic Wife, Three Kids, and No Intentions of Giving it Up had arrived for business - as usual.

'What's this I hear about a deal with the United States and Mexico?' he laughed, slapping "It" on the shoulder, if you could call it a shoulder. "It" was polymorphous at best.

"It" quivered, because "It" was excited and because "It"

had been slapped - sending shock waves through "It's" gelatinous structure. "It", of course, was too dim-witted to wonder how White Corporate Fellow with Heavy Briefcase, Alcoholic Wife, Three Kids, and No Intentions of Giving it Up could have known about a top-secret call from the President that occurred just a few minutes ago. But the White Corporate Fellow with Heavy Briefcase, Alcoholic Wife, Three Kids, and No Intentions of Giving it Up, sensing the assistant's curiosity - and catching a suspicious upward glance from The Young North American Indian Environmentalist Fellow, still sprawled across the floor - explained himself in due time.

As it turned out, the White Corporate Fellow with Heavy Briefcase, Alcoholic Wife, Three Kids, and No Intentions of Giving it Up had "It's" telephone tapped. When he heard about the deal, being an honest businessman, he simply had to make sure he'd get his fare share. Rifling through "It's" desk, which was pretty much empty, he didn't bother to pursue his case further or make any concrete demands whatsoever. He felt assured that just by making an appearance he'd benefit accordingly. Besides, further negotiations with "It" would be difficult and time consuming, to say the least.

In fact, if the truth be known, he didn't even like being near "It". He wished he hadn't touched "It". Now he would have to get his Armani dry-cleaned. Ignoring the assistant, stepping over The Young North American Indian Environmentalist Fellow, he made his way out. At dinner, later that day, he'd tell his relatives how disgusted he was by "It", just to get on their good side. He'd tell the same story to his workers at the factory the next morning. Of course, to him, the workers and his relatives were one-in-the-same, because all his relatives were working for him.

Now that White Corporate Fellow with Heavy Briefcase, Alcoholic Wife, Three Kids, and No Intentions of Giving it Up had left, "It" could finally relax. Some relaxation was long overdue. The assistant, sensing "It's" fatigue, helped The Young North American Indian Environmentalist Fellow up and showed him out. The assistant encouraged him to make a future appointment, or to bring matters up in the House of Commons, if he had a grievance. But, at the same time, the assistant warned him about getting too optimistic about his position. The Young North American Indian

Environmentalist Fellow, in a daze, just nodded, not knowing what else to do, letting his feet carry him blindly down the hallway.

The assistant turned to "It", as he usually did at the end of a hard day's work. Quite often, they'd discuss, in the loosest meaning of the word, the day's events and plan upcoming events. But "It" appeared to be asleep. Of course, it was very hard to tell, since "It" was devoid of eyes or eyelids and made no sounds whatsoever, let alone breathing - which no one knew how "It" managed. The assistant decided to leave "It" alone and head out.

Is "It" asleep or awake? Alert or subdued? Effective or just *there*? These were the questions that coursed through the assistant's head, as he closed the doors to "It's" office, sighing deeply. He couldn't help but think that his thoughts were shared by all Canadians. But, then again, they voted for "It".

The Trial

Lying in bed, wrapped tightly for warmth, surrounded by darkness, he felt the great comfort associated with familiar surroundings. Nothing was out of place and the routine was the same every night. Any change would only make sleep more difficult.

As usual, his thoughts turned to her. They were vivid enough to supply additional comfort, but somehow tangible enough to drive sleep further away. This quality caught him off-guard. He thought he was imagining it, but it was far too obvious and growing stronger and stronger. He lifted his head from the pillow, sniffing several times. It was definitely perfume. His nose turned slowly towards the source. His eyes adjusting to the darkness, he vaguely made out the pattern: red and white polka-dots seated in his chair, just three feet from where he lay.

He could see her quite clearly now. She had dark wavy hair, not quite shoulder length. However, since she was facing the other way, he could not identify her. She seemed to be nodding her head, but he did not know why. It was as if she was carrying on a conversation with someone. He lifted his head higher, still wrapped tightly in the sheets. Shaking his head, he questioned his state of mind. Was he mistaken? No, it rose up again from the darkness. He strained to hear. It was definitely a man's voice, slowly becoming more audible, as if approaching from a far corner. Squinting, hoping his other senses would confirm what he heard, he saw a faint image. Was he seeing things? Considering his state of mind - exhausted, expecting sleep, senses strained - it could have been what he *wanted* to see. Yet, it *did* look like a man before her, fading in and out of view, as he paced back and forth in the darkness.

Who was this stranger in his bedroom? He felt violated - threatened. What was the connection between the stranger and the girl?

All thoughts quickly turned away. The movement of his bed distracted him. An antique, it was prone to creaking at the slightest movement; he had grown accustomed to it long ago. It had been jiggling for quite some time, but now it seemed someone was trying to push the bed across the floor. The legs were scrapping the tiling.

Turning, he saw several solemn faces seated in chairs alongside the bed. With their backs against the wall, and the metal frame pressed to their legs, they were unable to tolerate the cramped conditions. In a group effort, they pushed him further away, as they saw fit. This allowed for more leg room, but such shenanigans made it impossible for him to pay attention, let alone sleep. Angered, he studied their faces. His eyes became accustomed - slowly, as if a dimmer switch was turning on. They all looked so weary, and unsympathetic to the fact he was trying to sleep. It was as if they were directing their anger and frustration directly at him, when it should be the other way around. They had made the intrusion on *him,* at such an hour; it was *his* room and he had every right to be upset.

Dazed, confused, and tired, he really didn't know what to do. Slowly, he turned away from the people seated alongside the bed. The scent of perfume still floated over him, but the girl's identity remained a complete mystery. Looking towards her, he realized his mind wasn't playing tricks on him after all. A tall man in a gray suit *was* standing before her, nodding as she spoke faintly. The man looked down at him with contempt. This late night visitation stirred his curiosity. He threw back the covers, intending to set the matter straight. But he no longer felt comfortable. Lying there, exposed, his surroundings seemed strange to him.

As the illumination within the room grew and grew, he saw guards, railings, chairs, desks, and benches. None of this was right. Where was *his* furniture? What happened to his personal belongings? Stranger still, his room wasn't *that* large. When the darkness completely receded, he realized he was before a judge, seated high atop the bench, with the jurors pressed in behind his bed. Now it was obvious: the girl was on trial before him, for some unknown reason. His curiosity reached an apex. What was her crime? How would it affect him?

"So kind of you to finally join us," the tall man in the gray suit said, turning away from the girl, "We apologize if we've inconvenienced you, but maybe now you'll cooperate and let justice run its course. How do you plead?"

"What was that?" he rubbed his eyes.

"These are very serious allegations!" the man raised his voice, shaking a finger at him. "How do you plead? Haven't you been paying attention?"

"How is this possible?" he thought aloud, scratching his head. The realization was almost too much for him. *He* was the one being tried, not the girl, and the tall man in the gray suit was the prosecutor.

"Your honour," the prosecutor approached the judge, "this is representative of the neglect and ignorance which my client has complained of. We want to make sure that this point is taken into account and included in the records."

"Request granted," the judge nodded. "Let it be known that the defendant has once again conspired against the plaintiff. Approach the bench," the judge motioned for him to step forward. "It is necessary to brief him, under the circumstances; he's missed the opening arguments."

Still lying in bed, he looked dumbly on, only seeing the girl's back and the prosecutor's cold, probing stare. Behind him, the jurors appeared equally unsympathetic.

"Approach the bench or a bailiff will escort you!" the judge roared.

"For once in your life, cooperate!" the prosecutor snarled, crossing his arms.

He got up and slowly approached the bench. The tiling was cold on his bare feet and his pyjamas provided little protection against the cool breezes generated by the ceiling fans. He paused, turning to see the girl. She looked down. He shook his head. For the life of him, he did not recognize her, or have the faintest idea who she was.

"Keep going," the prosecutor prodded him, motioning towards the bench.

In front of the bench, he tried to establish an impression of complete innocence, coupled with inability to stand trial. Accordingly, he rubbed his eyes again - thoroughly - and threw in some yawning for good measure. He even tried a bit of stumbling, as if dizzy or stunned. Unfortunately, all his efforts were popular tricks children play on parents, so no one seemed to buy them.

"Since you are unaware of the charges being brought against you," the judge began, "I will request that the court recorder read them back to you."

"But this is ridiculous," he shrugged, reaching under his pyjamas to scratch his shoulder. "What significance can this have when I don't even know her - the so called plaintiff?"

The prosecutor shook his head and smiled. The girl broke into tears and the jurors broke into fits of mumbling.

"Silence!" the judge brought down his gavel. "This courtroom must be orderly and the defendant will remain silent until he has heard the charges against him."

"But how can there be charges from a woman I've never met?" he glanced at the girl, her face hidden, still staring at the floor. "And moreover, what's more innocent than a man standing before a court in his pyjamas? I demand an explanation of all this. I'm expected at work tomorrow morning and I need my rest."

"Silence!" the judge brought the gavel down repeatedly. "You'll get your explanation in the form of a long list of charges against you, which may include contempt of court, if you persist with interrupting the proceedings."

The judge motioned to the recorder.

"The plaintiff," the recorder read from her notes, "who is too embarrassed to be identified, has charged the defendant, the man in the pyjamas, with several accounts of not returning phone calls, two accounts of broken dinner arrangements, one account of refusing to meet parents, and multiple accounts of general ignorance and indifference. The prosecution is calling for a life sentence, beginning with engagement and a three week honeymoon in New Zealand."

"How do you plead?" the judge looked down at him.

The jury stirred.

"This is insane," he shook his head.

"Answer the question," the judge fumed. "How do you plead to the charges you've just heard?"

"But I tell you," he insisted, "I don't even know her; I've had only the most general inkling she ever existed until now."

"Your honour," the prosecutor stepped forward, "we have a hostile defendant!"

The jury became quite agitated. Some of them stood up and hissed.

"Order! Order!" the judge banged his gavel, until he was red in the face. "No more outbreaks or I'll clear the court! Now, I could have the bailiff cart you out of here right now," he leaned over his bench, pointing a finger down at the defendant. "How do you plead?"

"Well, where's my lawyer?" he shrugged. "I mean, everything seems to be up and running, except for the most important detail - my defence!"

"Your lawyer was here an hour ago," the prosecutor began. "But seeing that you were asleep, he refused to wait and left. Now answer the judge: how do you plead? Another delay and I'll see that …"

"NOT GUILTY!"

The courtroom itself seemed to gasp. Jurors jumped up from their chairs. The judge banged his gavel and the bailiff rushed over to maintain order. Was it the late hour that got the jury so riled?

"How can I be anything but *not guilty*?" he hollered above the commotion. "I defy her to look me in the eye and tell me that she knows me!"

"You stay away from my client!" the prosecutor leaped in front of her. "Your honour, I recommend he be restrained."

"What possible threat can a man in his pyjamas pose?" he argued, looking towards the judge. "I have no weapons or bad intentions towards anyone."

"I don't want to hear about it," the prosecutor waved his hand, shaking his head. "I think you're disgusting. Look, you've made her cry again. How can someone be so insensitive?"

The jurors were in a rage. The bailiff drew his gun and waved it above their heads. Only then did they calm down.

"Your honour," the prosecutor approached the bench, "I'm afraid I must insist that the bailiff restrain the defendant. He should not be allowed to roam the courtroom freely."

"Request denied" the judge shook his head. "It's his bedroom; besides, he can't go far in his pyjamas. Let's get on with it, shall we? Are you prepared to give your defending statements?"

"I'm as ready as I'll ever be," he sighed, glancing around the courtroom, "given the circumstances."

"Proceed."

He paced in front of the jurors, trying to look as professional as he could, considering he was in his pyjamas. The pyjamas were a loose fit, so he had to keep pulling them up. But he wasn't about to let that get in his way.

"As I have said already," he began, "I do not know this woman. I do not know why she has charged me, but I am sure she is a good person who means no harm. The fact that she cannot look me in the face proves beyond a doubt she doesn't know me and her claims are false."

"Objection, your honour," the prosecutor interjected. "My client will not look him in the face because she ... because she is thinking about what kind of carpeting she would like best."

"Objection over-ruled," the judge sighed. "It's ridiculous and unprofessional to assume you can read your client's mind."

"But she is about to get married," the prosecutor motioned to her, "and carpeting is important."

"Very well," the judge sat back, "if you must persist along these lines. Miss, are you *really* thinking about carpeting?"

She did not answer, aside from sobbing lightly, nor did she look up from the floor.

"Obviously your client is being equally difficult," the judge crossed his arms. "Objection is still over ruled. The defendant may continue."

"Thank you, your honour," he nodded, eager to continue. "I think everyone here will agree that this is a complete embarrassment to me and the young lady before me. Accusations have been brought to light that have no merit whatsoever. How they came about, I don't know. But I can hardly be found guilty for not calling a person I don't even know. And while I admit that I had the faintest inkling she did exist, I cannot be found guilty of being ignorant or malicious under such circumstances. There just isn't any tangible evidence to convict me. I only hope the jury will understand the confusion and embarrassment I am suffering, and no doubt the young lady feels the same. I plead that the charges be dropped altogether."

"How can you stand there and say you had the faintest inkling that I exist!" she suddenly burst, looking up from the floor. "I am *real* and I am right *here!*"

The prosecutor comforted her. She left a courtroom full of damning silence in her wake.

"You stay back!" the prosecutor warned him, even though he remained perfectly motionless. "Haven't you done enough damage? Have you no shame? Your honour, surely it is apparent that the defendant must explain this *inkling* he had regarding my client's existence. I think he knows her all too well, and I am hereby charging him with contempt of court!"

"How do you plead to this new charge," the judge glared down at him.

He didn't know what to say, with this new development. But he couldn't help thinking that the entire case, and the courtroom itself, was highly unorganized, because they had yet to ask him to take an oath. Regardless, he answered honestly.

"I admit that I know her, but only under the vaguest circumstances imaginable."

"Explain yourself," the prosecutor demanded.

"I have thought of her," he hesitated, "or at least I think it was her, because I can never be sure whether she's really there or not. Under these circumstances, however, there was never any agreement regarding telephone calls, dinner arrangements, or visiting parents, because no real relationship existed, nor could it exist. If anything, it isn't *me* that's being put under trial, but my thoughts."

The jury became puzzled. Their quiet mumbling and curious looks were testament to that.

"I admire your attempt at confusing this court," the prosecutor laughed; "at this late hour, it seems highly possible. But you won't get off that easily. The sword of justice is clean and cuts a neatly defined path. Your thoughts dictate your actions, and the young lady seated, crying before you, is obviously very real. You are guilty on all charges and I demand that you be sentenced accordingly!"

Opinion was not in his favour. The jury nodded and the judge glared down at him. Even the bailiff shook his head, as if to say the defence was futile.

"Your honour," he took a deep breath, looking down at his feet, "may I approach the bench?"

"You may."

The prosecutor followed him forward.

"Your honour," he began nervously, "under the circumstances, without my lawyer present and wishing to get this over with, I'm willing to plea bargain."

"Go ahead," the judge nodded.

There was a brief pause, before he had collected himself enough to speak.

"I'm willing to plead guilty to the lesser charges of ignorance and indifference, providing that I be sentenced to dinner and a movie."

"Unacceptable," the prosecutor shook his head. "Look at her over there! Look at the state she's in! I've got the jury on my side and I could convict on a lot more than that!"

"What are your new terms?" the judge asked the prosecutor.

"We want dinner and a movie as starters," the prosecutor answered, "followed by six months of long walks, visits to the cottage, and possibly some theatre thrown in for good measure. Also, I recommend that the accused be placed under probation for six months, so he can't meet any other women."

"What kind of a person do you think I am?" he cried. "Do you really think I go chasing after women? I haven't dated in over five months and now I'm beginning to realize why! And I don't like the theatre!"

"Comments like that will get you into court time and time again," the judge warned him. "You've heard the reduced sentence, do you accept it?"

"I don't know," he rubbed the back of his neck, shaking his head. "You've caught me at a bad time. I'm tired and I can't recall what I have planned for the next few months. I don't have my day planner with me."

"Do you accept the reduced sentence?" the judge leaned over the bench.

"It's best that you do," the prosecutor crossed his arms.

"Oh, all right," he threw his arms up. "I just want to get back to bed."

The judge informed the jury that a decision had been made without the need for their verdict. This angered a lot of them, considering the hours they had to keep and the cramped conditions within the room. As the courtroom cleared, the bailiff led him back to bed and tucked him in.

"You should consider yourself lucky," the bailiff patted him on the head; "she's very attractive."

"Yes, she is," he sighed. "What time do you have there?"

"3:00 am."

"And I have to work tomorrow," he turned his head, closing his eyes.

He thought briefly of good restaurants and films. Maybe it wasn't so bad after all. She was very attractive, and she used such a creative way of getting his attention. He actually became optimistic about his sentence. It filled him with a certain comfort, allowing him to relax, despite it all. Drifting off, almost dreaming, he suddenly jerked back the covers and stood up. He forgot to get her phone number.

How to Keep Cats Out of Your Garbage

Life is full of ups and downs, but nothing is worst than cats in your garbage. However, unlike life, garbage mining cats can be easily dealt with. All it takes is some time, a bit of thought, a balloon, and some bacon grease.

Simply inflate the balloon and spread the bacon grease all over it. Once it is fully coated, carefully place the balloon inside the garbage can - with the lid off, so the cats can obtain easy access to it. Remember to target the garbage can that historically attracts the most cats. Then go to bed, resting assured that you will no longer be awakening to spilt garbage.

While you sleep, the irresistible aroma of bacon grease will waft through the neighbourhood, undoubtedly attracting trouble-making cats. When they encounter the balloon, pure instinct will drive them to lick it. This quickly escalates to biting. Before they know it, the balloon bursts, sending cats scurrying for cover. From that moment on, the cats' interest will no longer be sufficient enough to justify a return visit.

If, by chance, you find this method doesn't work, then switch from bacon grease to fish oil or cream cheese - whatever suits the particular tastes of troublesome cats in your neighbourhood. This method is also moderately effective against unwanted relatives.

The Future, a Radio, and a Travelling Salesperson

Quite suddenly, and inexplicably, he wondered what the future held. Looking at his watch, he discovered he was six foot three. In a panic, he set down his coffee and grabbed his briefcase. He didn't know he was that tall, but he was always three feet from every appointment. If his boss was feeling less than sympathetic, he might end up being fired because of it. Yes, without question, he had to make haste.

With the briefcase full of displays and test models, he raced to his next scheduled client: an old woman who lived alone with her radio. The other employees had told him all about her radio. As it turned out, the radio made a good companion for her; it rarely shed and only once in awhile, in an act of sudden playfulness, would it chase the mailman from the property. Luckily, its cord was not long enough to make it around the corner, so the mailman didn't have to go far to seek safety.

It didn't take him long to reach the old woman's house, or so he thought. Knocking on the door, he was immediately greeted by the radio, awakened from its deep sleep. He feared repercussions; he could hear its static hiss on the other side of the door. Checking his watch, he was six foot five.

"Well," he sighed, having ran all the way over, "only two inches; that's not too bad."

He felt secure his boss wouldn't mind these few extra inches, although he'd have a hard time getting through the front door when he returned to the office at the end of the day. Just as he was about to knock again, the door opened. The old woman, a scowl across her face, looked him up and down.

"You're tall!" she snapped, obviously irritated. "You were supposed to be six foot three!"

"I'm so sorry about this," he rushed to explain, "I was in the cafe, enjoying my break after a long day's work, when I lost track of my height."

"Well, come on in," she groaned, pushing the radio aside with her foot, so he could pass. The radio, feeling defiant in the presence of a stranger, let out an old jazz number.

"That's a nice radio you have there," he remarked, trying to get on her good side, in order to insure a sale.

"My grandson bought it for me, last Christmas. God damned thing - it's a nuisance!"

"Well I don't know about that," he argued politely, petting the radio, which was now rubbing up against his leg. "It actually seems very well-mannered and affectionate."

"Not the radio," she cried, "my grandson! God damn nuisance - face like a pig, and as useful as the sleeves on a vest! Come to think of it," she rubbed her chin, "I once knitted him a vest with sleeves, and do you think he could tell the difference? Of course not!"

"That's really interesting," he quickly interjected, using his skill as a fast-talking salesman to get the deal in motion, "but before I get any taller, I have a wide assortment of watches to show to you."

"Watches!" she laughed aloud. "What the hell do I need a watch for? My height hasn't changed in the last 30 years! In fact, I think I'm shrinking! It would be useless for me to buy something like that now. Why, if I didn't have one foot in the grave, I'd be free to kick the bucket right now!"

The old woman laughed for what was quickly becoming an inappropriate length of time. He knew it was going to be a hard sell; morbid old people always were. Yet, he did not want to return to the office empty-handed. It was time for action, before his purpose was crushed by laughter.

"Well," he suddenly blurted, "you could buy a watch right now and if you kick the bucket tomorrow, or perhaps shortly after I leave, you could leave it to your grandson."

The old woman suddenly stopped laughing. She gave him a serious look, making him feel very uncomfortable. He couldn't believe what he had just said; only a long, hard day could be blamed for letting a line like that slide. The back of his neck became sticky. He could see himself racing out the door with his tail between his legs, the radio in hot pursuit - obituaries blaring from its speaker. She was motioning for him to come closer. He slowly, reluctantly, leaned towards her; she was an old woman, but she looked like she could pack a wallop. He could hardly keep his eyes open; his face was hot with the fear of reprisal. Taking his collar, a stern look on her face, she drew him even closer, so she could speak directly into his ear. He squinted, shrugging his shoulders, preparing for the inevitable.

"Would you massage my feet?" she asked.

"Well," he paused, shocked at the request, "I guess. I guess I could."

The old woman sat down in a comfortable chair, indicating that she expected prompt service. He didn't know what to make of the situation; he wasn't keen on massaging her feet, but, all things considered, perhaps he could still salvage a sale if he went through with it. To add to his dilemma, and general state of confusion, the radio leaped up onto the window sill and began to blast a weather report.

"Must be a cat in the garden," the old woman grumbled, taking off her slippers.

While still seated in her chair, the old woman called out directions to him, as he searched throughout the house for various needful things. Returning with towels, baby oil, warm water, and a magazine for her to read, he set to work.

"How did you get so tall?" she asked quite suddenly, setting down her magazine, after a prolonged moment of uncomfortable silence.

"I was at the cafe," he answered abruptly, not being in a mood to converse.

"Doing what?"

"Not too much," he mumbled, massaging her ankles, "I was just wondering about my future."

"What's the matter, don't like being a travelling salesperson?"

"No I don't, as a matter of fact," he spoke with some enthusiasm, now that he had someone to listen to his troubles. "I've been a salesperson for far too long."

"How long?"

"Oh, about three feet."

"You've really grown with the company then," she began to rock in her chair, making the massage even more of a task for him.

"I suppose so," he sighed.

"So what does your future hold?" she asked, watching him apply more oil to her feet.

"I don't know," he shook his head. "I just can't see myself at seven foot two."

Suddenly, the old woman became visibly saddened. She stopped rocking in her chair; she looked as if she was going to cry. Out of concern, he stopped massaging her feet.

"Seven foot two," she said, with a far-off voice, "that was my husband's height when he passed away."

"Oh, I'm so sorry," he apologized, clasping her hand. He felt like a heel for saying the wrong thing once again, even though he had spoken with the utmost innocence, and with the best intentions.

"I'm over it now," she began, "please continue with the massage, and hand me a towel to get this oil off my hand. Yes," she shook her head, wiping the oil from her hand, "it's hard to forget the loss of a loved one. He had a history of heart problems, and he was in a plane at the time, you see. I had always warned him about planes, and all his smoking and drinking, but he wouldn't listen. He began to suffer a heart attack, with no medical help on board. You see, the plane was full of circus performers. In all the chaos, a fanatical Moslem extremist mistook him for the British Minister of Defence and stabbed him in the back repeatedly. When he realised his mistake, he apologized to my husband and helped him back into his chair. Moments later, a Bengal tiger broke loose of its cage, back in the cargo bay, and raced into the cabin, mauling my husband beyond recognition. At that moment, the pilot accidently swallowed a bottle of Scotch. In a fit of blind rage, he crashed the plane into a bridge. My husband, the only survivor, but weakened by his ordeal, crawled out from the wreckage and was run over by a car full of drunken youths, who had just crashed through a barricade. You see, the bridge was blocked off, because it was set for demolition at that very moment. They tried to warn those youths, but it was too late. The bridge went up in a puff of smoke and my poor husband ended up in the river. He's not a strong swimmer, you know, but he managed to flop ashore, some few hundred kilometres downstream. As luck would have it, a group of picnickers, some of them young medical students, rushed to his aid. Since he was famished after his ordeal, one of the young students gave him a bite of her chicken salad sandwich. He died soon afterwards, on route to the hospital. The coroner, upon investigating the cause of death, discovered that the sandwich the young student fed him was contaminated by Streptococcus bacteria. Yes, it was the chicken salad sandwich that did him in."

There was a moment of silence, as he digested the incredible tale she had just served up. He had no reason not to believe her; she was genuinely saddened by it all.

"I don't know what to say," he shook his head in bewilderment, having stopped the massaging to listen carefully. "I had no idea that you'd been through so much with the loss of your husband and all. And to think that I came over here with the sole, selfish intent of making a sale to someone as lovely as yourself, who deeply regrets the loss of a loved one, who must live her final days alone with her radio."

"It's a tough break," she shrugged, "but I've gotten used to the long lonely days. That's why I greatly appreciate it when so much as a salesman comes around, especially yourself - you give such a good massage. But I suppose you must be going now."

"Yes," he replied, "it's getting tall. But before I go, I'd like you to have this lovely watch - completely free of charge, of course!"

"Why, you're too kind," she smiled, showing him to the door. The radio could no longer be bothered with the comings and goings of strangers; asleep in the far corner, you could hear its gentle humming.

"But I really don't know what I can do with a watch now," she continued, "although I was a giant in my time."

"Well, it's the least I can do," he explained, "to make up for having bothered you with my pettiness. I must remember," he paused just outside the door, "to be more considerate with my clients, and less selfish. Of course, it would help if I could sell a few watches in the process!"

"You shouldn't worry yourself with such thoughts," the old lady laughed. "You're young and full of life! You've got many more inches ahead of you, before you reach the height of your career, so don't get all wrapped up about your future at this point. Besides, everyone has the same future ahead of them anyway."

"Oh really?" he began, being rather interested in the topic, as of late. "Well then, what is this common future we all share?"

"Well," she laughed, pointing at his watch, "we all end up six feet under!"

A True Story About a Monkey

Two research scientists once worked in a top secret underground facility where they conducted some of the earliest behavioural experiments on monkeys. In one such experiment, they confined a monkey to a vast room with only two fixtures: an overhead observation light and a banana. The banana was hanging down from the ceiling, so it was six feet off the ground. The two scientists watched eagerly from behind the locked door, peering in through the small window. As the day unfolded, they paid close attention, noting the monkey's hunger response. But there was no noticeable response. He made no attempt to reach the banana; in fact, he didn't seem to acknowledge it at all. Sitting right below it, unmoving, it was as if he was purposely ignoring the banana. This left the scientists perplexed. Of course, it was impossible for the monkey to reach the banana, but why had he made no effort at all? In fact, why no movement - not even a glance upwards? Was the monkey's sense of defeat so strong that it rendered him immobile? The monkey remained in the room over night for further observation, with the hopes his hunger response would kick in. Still nothing happened.

The next day, one of the scientists got a bright idea. There were many boxes around the facility, so he suggested they throw some in and see if the monkey was intelligent enough to stack them and climb up to the banana. The two agreed on the plan, brought the boxes in, carefully scattered them around the monkey, and left the room, locking the door behind them. The monkey showed absolutely no response to their brief visit - or the boxes. Exhausted and hungry from their long hours of observation, the two scientists left to get some lunch. When they returned, they peered into the room. Sure enough, the monkey had eaten all the boxes.

Rumours

"Sticks and stones may break my bones, but names will never hurt me!"

Whoever came up with that saying has obviously never been the victim of merciless gossip and innuendo. I'm talking about the sort of rumours and backstabbing that gnaw at the very soul like a Rottweiler ravaging a honey baked ham.

Let's face it - cuts and bruises heal, but hurtful words never leave the deepest recesses of our subconscious. In this regard, the pen really is mightier than the sword. Before I get too carried away (it is already sufficiently obvious that I deplore gossip, mean spirited or otherwise), let me quickly switch to how all this is affecting me. For as of late, I have been the victim of an intense smear campaign birthed by equal parts ignorance, jealousy, spite, dishonesty, and misrepresentation of the basic facts. I will now use this opportunity to clear the matter up – once and for all. Read this carefully – without prejudice.

During the summer of 2003, I decided to vacation in South America. The name of my country of destination will remain anonymous. Suffice to say that I had just completed my Masters Degree and was anxious to relax. I was also looking forward to leaving Toronto, where my social life at the time was not worth mentioning, and travelling abroad to meet new and exciting people. I had mentally prepared myself to "let loose" and have a great time – forgetting all the problems, constraints, and inhibitions of a North American lifestyle. As I flew over anonymous mountains, my mind reeled with the possibilities. Suddenly, alarm spread throughout the plane. People were screaming and yelling in a foreign tongue. I could feel the pressure change. My stomach knotted. I could hardly come to grips with what was happening, but the facts were unavoidable. The plane was rocketing back towards earth. I could see mountains flashing by. We were going to crash.

About one hour later, I woke up. Miraculously, I was not injured. I was still seated in my section, but my section – or what remained of it - was completely separated from the rest of the debris littered around the mountain. No one else was as fortunate. I was the sole survivor. Before I go any further, let me restate that I wish to set the record straight, once and for all. I beg your understanding in this matter. Let the following statement serve as both the end of this narrative and an end to the vicious rumours and misinformation surrounding me.

It was cold as hell up on that mountain. I had no way of contacting help. How was I to know that a rescue team would be there in only two hours? I'm telling you – I had to eat those people!

As the Crow Flies

Benjamin awoke suddenly, after fitful sleep. His shoulders ached. Perhaps he hadn't slept at all. Rubbing his eyes, straining, he tried in vain to read the clock perched on his desk, at the foot of his bed, by the window. But the light from a few lonely stars outside was not adequate, and it didn't help any that he was without his glasses. Angered at awaking, letting curiosity get the best of him, he pushed himself up and leaned towards the clock for a closer look. A beak snapped at his forehead. Wings flapped wildly in the darkness.

Pulling away, he flung an arm up in defence, unable to see the source of the attack. Yet, no further attack occurred. Lowering his arm, hearing a subtle caw, his eyes somewhat adjusted now, he noticed a large black crow sitting atop his clock, shrouded in the darkness.

The limited starlight found its way through the window and reflected off the crow's blackened feathers. The crow fluttered his wings, perhaps out of force of habit. His eyes, like black marbles, rolled and winked with each twitch of his head. Benjamin was able to get a good view of the crow in the dim light, yet, for the life of him, he couldn't see what time it was.

Feeling under his bed, where he always kept his glasses when he slept, he found nothing. Perhaps the crow, crows being notorious pests and known to be attracted to shiny objects, had flown off with them, hiding them in some tall tree.

Motivated by both curiosity and impatience with his late night visitor, Benjamin leaned towards his clock, demanding to know the time at any cost. Again the crow snapped at him. He lunged for the bird, hoping to scare it off. The bird, quite large and intimidating in the darkness, flapped and cawed, talons gripping the clock, almost flying up to the ceiling with it.

"Benjamin," a familiar voice floated through his locked door. The crow, clock held tight, landed back on the desk, "are you alright in there?"

It was Benjamin's mother, standing outside his door, in the lit hallway. He could see the shadow of her feet through the bottom of the door. The crow called out again, as if to answer for him, but more than likely just to create a stir, characteristic of his species.

"Benjamin?" she persisted, still knocking.

"What's wrong with him now?" came an unfamiliar female voice, running from the kitchen, knocking into a picture on the wall, causing it to sway like a pendulum. It was a portrait of a very young boy, standing in a garden.

"Sounds like he's got a bird in there," he heard his mother whisper to the stranger. "I hope it doesn't ruin the curtains!"

"Oh Benjamin," the stranger cried, "are you alright in there?"

"Benjamin," his mother called, knocking again, "please don't be difficult. We're worried sick."

"I'm fine," Benjamin called back, perturbed. He didn't understand their concern, nor could he explain the presence of a strange female voice outside if his room, apparently someone who knew his mother though. "I just awoke to check the time." He threw back the covers.

"What's going on out there?" he heard his father's voice, originating from the sitting room. "I'm trying to watch the game. I have to pay attention. I've got money on it. I joined the hockey pool at work."

Benjamin thought he heard a young boy cry out with glee. He could hear toys crashing together.

"He won't come out," his mother called back to his father, "and he's making a lot of noise in there. It's strange."

"Benjamin," the voice of the stranger pleaded, trying the locked door, "please, what's wrong? Please come out. I'm worried."

"Look what you've done," his father's voice boomed from the sitting room. There must have been a commercial, because he began quite the spiel. "The entire family in an uproar!" he opened a new bottle of beer, still seated in his favourite chair. "Just come out now, Benjamin. Don't get into one of your moods. Look how upset Francine is, and it's your fifth anniversary, for crying out loud! Whoops, the game's back on!"

Benjamin remained silent, digesting everything that was said. He had forgotten completely about the time now; curiosity led him down a different path. What was this talk of an anniversary? It was strange, he couldn't explain it. Shaking sleep away, he suddenly felt very alien. Confused, he unlocked his door and opened it. He was greeted by a warm embrace from an attractive young woman.

"I was so worried," she kissed him gently.

"Here he is now," mother called to the father, as if he was listening in on the progress from his chair in the sitting room, television blaring.

Suddenly, there was the sound of breaking glass.

"Oh no," the mysterious woman drew her arms away from Benjamin and covered her mouth, "it's fallen! I knocked into it by accident."

"Don't worry yourself," mother walked towards it, "I'll clean it up."

Benjamin's thoughts were jumbled. It was bad enough that he'd just been awakened, not from the best sleep either, but now he was confronted by just too many perplexing factors, all intertwined. Firstly, he didn't recognize the hallway outside of his own room. It was narrower, more claustrophobic, poorly lit, compared to his real home. Secondly, his mother, it struck him, had become much older - over night, it seemed. And thirdly, most importantly, who was this woman embracing him, looking deep into his eyes for some sign of recognition? Was this the Francine his father had shouted about? And the talk of an anniversary? Was this his so-called wife?

"What's happening to me?" he thought aloud.

"What's wrong with you?" Francine shrunk back. "Are you well? I thought the sleep would help."

Obviously, his eyes could not lie, especially not to a woman who loved him, or so it seemed. She saw the lack of recognition, the confusion, and, unfortunately, it formed a massive cold front passing over her. But how could he be blamed? He was an innocent dreamer, plunged into strange circumstance, without any explanation or warning. Benjamin's thoughts disappeared. He was struck by a strong, unusual recognition, bringing back memories of his own childhood photos. The young boy, previously in the sitting room with Benjamin's father, waddled forth. Was it possible?

Francine went over and picked him up, bringing him towards Benjamin. He was an attractive boy, but with the smile of a trouble maker. Yes it was possible; after all, Benjamin's own mother always said he was a terror when he was young. The boy looked up at him with the look of someone who had just recognized a kindred spirit. It didn't surprise Benjamin; he'd felt it himself, but kept it at bay; one of his more far-fetched explanations. Yet, a child is more receptive to the unusual and the fantastic than an adult. This is why the boy had that wicked little grin, that look of sharing a secret only with his father and no one else.

Suddenly, there was a loud hissing in the background.

"Oh," Francine cried, "the soup! I forgot about it."

The young boy in her arms, she hurried into the kitchen to turn down the heat. Benjamin's mother helped her clean up the mess that boiled over, soiling the stove and the floor. The distraction saved Benjamin from further scrutiny. But he was far from feeling safe and comfortable. Wandering into the sitting room, his father, also significantly older now, sat in front of the television, sipping beer and cheering on his team. The sitting room was small and dingy, poorly furnished compared to what Benjamin was accustomed to. The cheap paintings on the wall, the dusty lamps, the scratched furniture - absolutely none of it was familiar to him.

"This place," he blurted, "I don't feel comfortable here."

"What was that?" his mother came out from the kitchen, followed by Francine and the young boy, throwing himself on his toys.

Benjamin did not wish to be cruel. His predicament seemed impossible - beyond comprehension. As a result, he couldn't, in all fairness, direct his anger and impatience at his parents, or his supposed wife and son. Perhaps in vain, he tried to repair the damage his comment had made, in the process hoping to gain some insight into why things were as they were - or how things would be in his future. That was his official explanation.

"It's too small here," Benjamin motioned around him, "and dingy. I liked the old place the best. Lots of open space and wondrous antiques. I'm just not accustomed to anything else. It's such a shock for me."

"Oh Benjamin, why must you go on about it?" his mother cried. "Aren't you over it yet?"

"After all these years. Your poor mother!" father spoke up during a commercial. "You know it was hard for us to sell the old house. But the bills and the debts, it was just too much. And now, of all the times to dredge that up, you choose your anniversary! What terrible timing! You should have stayed in bed, rather than awakened with such an ugly disposition. We've all been through far too much in the last few years and you're well aware of it. You should be ashamed! Whoops, the game's back on!"

Benjamin rubbed his brow. His shoulders still ached. They ached since he awoke. However, now there were sharp stabbing pains, and an unrelenting itch. Feeling under his pyjamas, he discovered that his shoulders were deeply marked by talons. Yes, time flies, but it carries the dreamers with it, regardless of whether they're ready or not, and completely against their will.

"Benjamin," Francine interrupted his thoughts, taking his hand "why do you look at me that way? What's wrong with you? I thought a sleep would make you feel better."

Without warning, Benjamin pulled away from her and raced into the kitchen.

"What's wrong?" Francine called out to him.

"He was not easy to raise," his father sipped his beer, during a penalty announcement, "always distracted. Don't expect him to change any time soon. Maybe he wants some of that soup."

"This is just too much for me," Francine sat next to his mother on a quaint little sofa. She could hear Benjamin in the kitchen, apparently searching for something. She watched her son push about with his trucks and cars, uttering all sorts of imaginative noises. "I don't know what to do when he gets like this."

"Don't worry," Benjamin's mother consoled her, setting down her magazine, as Benjamin raced into the sitting room, looking around madly at walls and furniture, "it's just one of his phases; best to let it run its course. I'm sure it won't affect your relationship at all, having been married for five years now. You're through the worst of it - the first few years are always the worst. Besides, you make such a wonderful couple. You're definitely birds of a feather."

Benjamin's mother returned to her magazine, and Francine watched Benjamin closely, running around in his pyjamas like a madman. He grabbed his father's left wrist, then dropped it, looking disgusted. His father showed no reaction, glued to his game. He then came over and checked his mother's wrist, prying her away from her magazine, and then Francine's. She looked at him blankly, as he turned and sped off, racing through the halls, in and out of the bedrooms, slamming doors behind him. These odd habits worried her, but her son, excited by it all, and being very young, took off after his father to help him runabout madly, slamming doors. It was a son's duty.

Staring blankly at the television, Francine heard Benjamin return to the kitchen, searching through all the cupboards, cursing under his breath. He appeared at the door to the sitting room.

"I'm going back to bed now," he announced.

His son ran over and sat next to Francine. He smiled knowingly at Benjamin. To such a young mind, this was all playful fun. But to an adult, it was devastating. Benjamin leaned over Francine and kissed her good night, overcome by the feeling of kissing someone you're greatly attracted to but have only just met. A brief goodnight to his parents and he was ready. He looked at his son, not knowing what to think. But his son simply smiled and nodded, which was all he needed.

Returning to his room, locking his door, he stepped carefully back into bed, darkness all around him. Laying there, wrapped in blankets, he was furious that he was unable to find a single clock in the entire house - or even a calendar for that matter. There was a flap of wings. Yes, of course he was still there. He had to make his presence known. But Benjamin would ignore him now. He figured that whatever trick had plucked the crow from his dreams could just as easily return the bird. He just hoped it would be easy on his shoulders. Exhausted by the ordeal, he quickly succumbed.

He awoke suddenly after fitful sleep. His shoulders ached. It seemed like he hadn't slept at all. Rubbing his eyes, straining, he tried in vain to read the clock sitting on his desk, at the foot of his bed, by the window. But the light provided by a few lonely stars was not adequate, and it didn't help any that he was without his glasses. Angered at awaking, letting curiosity get the best of him, he pushed himself up and leaned towards the clock for a closer look. A beak snapped at his forehead, followed by a brush of wind caused by flapping wings. Pulling away, he flung an arm up in defence, unable to see the source of the attack. Yet, no further attack occurred. Lowering his arm, hearing a subtle caw, his eyes somewhat adjusted now, he noticed a large black crow sitting atop his clock, shrouded in the darkness.

What light was allowed through the window caused the crow's blackened feathers to shine as he fluttered his wings, perhaps out of force of habit. His eyes, like black marbles, rolled and winked at Benjamin with each twitch of his head. All this Benjamin could make out in the dim light, yet, for the life of him, he couldn't see what time it was! Feeling under his bed, where he always kept his glasses when he slept, he could not find them. Perhaps the crow, crows being notorious pests and known to be attracted to shiny objects, had flown off with them, hiding them in some tall tree.

Motivated by both curiosity and impatience with his late night visitor, again Benjamin leaned towards his clock, demanding to know the time at any cost. Again the crow snapped at him. He lunged for the bird, hoping only to scare it off. The bird, quite large and intimidating in the darkness, flapped and cawed, talons gripping the clock, almost flying up to the ceiling with it.

"Benjamin," a familiar voice floated through his locked door, as the crow, clock held tight, landed back on the desk, "are you alright in there?"

And then it struck Benjamin. He froze in his bed, momentarily, then jerked up and looked around. Was it possible? He had experienced spells like this before.

"Benjamin?" his mother called, still knocking.

"What's wrong with him now?" came another familiar voice, running from the kitchen.

"Sounds like he's got a bird in there," he heard his mother whisper. "I hope it doesn't ruin the curtains."

"Oh Benjamin," Francine cried, "are you alright in there?"

In a sudden burst of what might be called anger, brought on by a highly unusual circumstance that would justify a wide variety of emotions, he flung back his covers, causing the crow to leap up again.

"Straighten the picture in the hallway!" he hollered towards the locked door. Through the bottom of the door, he could see the shadows of the two figures in the hallway outside. "Do it before it falls and breaks," he continued, "and take your soup off the oven because it's about to boil over!"

There was a period of silence. He heard his mother and Francine move to the end of the hallway and then into the kitchen. He listened very carefully; nothing - no noise, no word - would slip by him. The crow, still atop the clock, flapped its wings impatiently. He waved a hand at it, as if to silence it, as if he had any control over this creature of the night who visits dreamers as he sees fit. Sure enough, straining to hear, his mother and his supposed wife ran back to his door. He could hear them whispering. Obviously they were amazed. He smiled to himself.

"Benjamin," his mother knocked, trying the lock as well, "please come out here. We're worried."

There was a pause, and then he heard whispering again. It sounded as though Francine was trying to coax his mother along.

"Benjamin," she knocked again, "you were right about the portrait and the soup on the oven. How did you do that? We'd really like you to come out now."

Benjamin laughed out loud. The crow cawed.

"I'm an aspiring Nostradamus!" he hollered, laughing. "I can see the future!"

Suddenly, he heard his father leap up from his chair in the sitting room and come running into the hallway. Apparently, he had been paying some attention to what was going on.

"Ask him if he knows who's going to win the game!" he hollered.

The young boy came running from the sitting room as well. He slid between his mother and the door.

"Daddy," he spoke through the key hole, "are you back again?"

Benjamin just laughed. There was little else he could do. It was a common reaction for someone under such a strain, such a strange series of events and realisations.

"Go back to Granddad," Francine took him by the arm.

"But I don't want to," the boy grumbled. "I want to run around the house some more."

"Go back!"

The boy left the door, reluctantly.

"Benjamin," his mother started up again, "maybe you should come out now. You've been sleeping for so long. Surely you feel better now."

"I'm a grown man," Benjamin shot back, "and I don't need to be told when to get out of bed. I'm staying here - and that's that!"

"What's come over him?" he heard Francine whisper to his mother.

"I don't know," she shrugged, "a phase of his. Best to let it run its course."

His mother led Francine back to the sitting room. Benjamin shifted around in his bed and suddenly felt a sharp pain in each shoulder. Slipping his fingers under his pyjamas, he discovered that the wounds were very deep now, beginning to burn.

"Well," Benjamin looked towards the crow, "I don't approve of your trickery. Why this place? Why again? I vaguely recall that I have things of importance to accomplish in the morning: some house chores, papers to review, calls to make. All those things I did before - when I was still a single, relatively happy young man. So why not just let me rest in peace?"

The crow looked at him blankly, as blankly as a crow can. His eyes, those black marbles, darted back and forth, still atop the clock, of course. Benjamin would think no more of it. How could he? It was all a terrible mistake, a mistake of the powers that be, of course - not his mistake. With this in mind, he allowed himself to drift off to sleep.

He awoke suddenly after fitful sleep. Of course he did! His shoulders ached. Why shouldn't they? It seemed like he hadn't slept at all. Rubbing his eyes, he was glad it was all over with. Other things concerned him now; so many things to do, first thing in the morning. Yet the sun was far from rising. Angered at awaking so early, straining, he tried in vain to read the clock sitting on his desk, at the foot of his bed, by the window. But the light provided by a few lonely stars outside was not adequate, and it didn't help any that he was without his glasses. Letting curiosity get the best of him, he pushed himself up and leaned towards the clock for a closer look. A beak snapped at his forehead, followed by a brush of wind caused by flapping wings. Pulling away, he fell to his pillow, sighing deeply.

"You again?" he grumbled.

The crow's eyes, like black marbles, rolled and winked at Benjamin with each twitch of his head. All this Benjamin could make out in the dim light, yet, for the life of him, he couldn't see what time it was! Of course he couldn't! And his glasses? Why bother checking! The bird, as large and intimidating as ever, in the darkness, flapped and cawed, talons gripping the clock, almost flying up to the ceiling with it.

"Benjamin," his mother's voice floated through his locked door, as the crow, clock held tight, landed back on the desk, "are you alright in there?"

Normally, the flight of the crow was predictable. But now the crow had grown unreliable, no longer to be trusted by travelling dreamers. Benjamin, lying quietly in bed, thought about it carefully, distracted somewhat by the pain in his shoulders, now quite severe. It seemed like the crow was circling something of interest, as crows often do. But why this particular point in time? It seemed of no consequence. Yet, he had learnt several things, all of them disheartening, rather bleak, and of debateable importance.

"Benjamin?" mother asked, still knocking.

"What's wrong with him now?" Francine came running from the kitchen.

Benjamin, ignoring the ruckus in the hallway, continued to reflect on the events. What significance did it all hold for him? He knew he'd be married, with a child, and his parents wouldn't be able to maintain the old house. But why did the crow keep bringing him back? Once was more than enough, and almost too much for him to handle as it was, being too tired and miserable to appreciate it fully.

"Sounds like he's got a bird in there," his mother whispered to Francine. "I hope it doesn't ruin the curtains."

"Oh Benjamin," Francine cried, "are you alright in there?"

"Benjamin," his mother called, knocking again, "please don't be difficult. We're worried sick."

Benjamin, still ignoring the pleading at his door, reached beneath his pyjamas and felt his shoulders. Blood trickled down from the wounds. It seemed unlikely that they'd heal. The fault of the crow, of course, but also the price that any dreamer must pay, a burden on his shoulders – but also the key to freedom. Benjamin didn't feel it was a price he should be paying. He wasn't enjoying the trip. How could he? How could the crow be so careless with its passenger? Why couldn't it let him off at the signing of the Declaration of Independence, or a nudist beach, or a combination thereof? Why not something exciting, memorable, something to be discussed over coffee at the office the next day? Why this same hell again and again?

"Benjamin," Francine pleaded, trying the locked door "please, what's wrong? Please come out. I'm worried."

"He won't come out," his mother called back to his father, in the sitting room, "and he's making a lot of noise in there. It's strange."

"Can't this wait for a commercial?" Father barked back.

Benjamin shook his head.

"Why," he thought aloud, whispering softly to the crow, "why are you doing this to me?"

Benjamin was surprised at how weary he suddenly became. In the comfort of his bed, shrouded in darkness, with the gentle flutter of the crow's wings, oblivious to the pain in his shoulders, he fell back to sleep.

In the morning, he awoke for the last time. The sun crept in through the window and over his desk, reflecting off the clock. Reaching under his bed, he found his glasses. Putting them on, he noticed it was eight o'clock. Slowly he pushed himself up out of bed; his shoulders were a mess now. Unlocking the door, leaving his room, he wandered down the hall. He paused in front of the portrait on the wall, a photograph of a handsome young man, his own son, now fully grown, standing in a garden. In the dim light of the hallway, and with the dark background in the portrait, he could see his own reflection superimposed over his son's. All the wrinkles, the grey hair, the weathered face of a man in his final years. Moving away from the portrait, somewhat saddened, he paused in the sitting room. He was alone, of course; he had been for the last ten years. No one else in that small house he'd inherited from his parents so many years ago.

Thinking back to the portrait, reflecting on his life, he hated the impudence of his youth, somewhere far in the past. He hated the selfishness and the lack of foresight, the preoccupation with unimportant things like office work and daily chores, obscuring all things that should be held dearest. But could his past self be blamed? After all, he didn't know what he knew now, so his reaction seemed warranted, if not justifiable.

Of course, he'd beg the crow to carry him back once again, but the sun was up, the rooster cried, and the crow was gone. No more chances; three was enough. He had failed. Obviously, he appreciated the past more than his past self appreciated it - or the future, for that matter. But it proved very difficult to get his past self to realise his folly. If only he could get through to him back then, that was the plan; then things would be different. But the feeling was so strong within him; he had such hope. How he strived to remember those simple moments of domestic bliss! Yes, come to think of it, he'd have went back a hundred times, but his past self, impatient and lacking the wisdom he now had, wouldn't allow it; too much of an inconvenience for him. Of course, all of this is insignificant to a bird that could drop you anywhere, whenever it tires, whenever it sees fit. No, he could not blame the crow.

Moving back down the hallway, towards his bedroom, all things considered, he was still thankful that he was given those last few opportunities. Closing the door behind him, locking it, he heard something at his window. It was the crow, on the outside looking in, beating and flapping against the pane of glass, perhaps craving his perch atop the clock. Benjamin slid slowly into bed, his shoulders aching from an age long burden of hopes and dreams. With his head resting on his pillow, they exchanged their final glances. The crow's black marble eyes blinked with each twitch of his head, his wings shot up, he let out a tremendous cry and then disappeared into the sky. Benjamin turned away from the window. No longer caring what time it was, he closed his eyes and fell into a deep, deep sleep.

A Note on Fancy Toffee Tins

When I was young, I had a pet hamster named Morton. I was very fond of Morton, but like all good things, he died one night. The next morning, I was left to deal with his demise. It was a harsh Ontario winter, but my father insisted that he'd dig a hole for Morton and bury him. So out he went, in his parka and boots, digging through two feet of snow and ice before coming anywhere close to the frozen soil.

My father was a dedicated man who liked to dig, but he didn't have much of a sense of ceremony. He said I could just wrap Morton in some paper towels and drop him into the hole. I insisted that wasn't good enough for my Morton. I went back into the house to look for something more appropriate. My mother made it clear that her Tupperware was off-limits. Searching through my room, the answer had been right before me all along.

On my desk, I had a fancy toffee tin which I kept all my notes, letters, and Canadian Tire money in. I emptied it without question; it had been called upon for a higher purpose. I went back outside, my father waiting for me at the hole. I said a few parting words, put Morton inside the fancy toffee tin, and carefully lowered him into the ground. My father said it looked good.

I was extremely proud to have given my beloved Morton a burial befitting a hamster of his status. And to this day, I must stress that if you have small pets, it's a good idea to keep those fancy toffee tins around.

The Package

"I have a package for you to sign for," the messenger announced, pen and clipboard outstretched.

"Hmm?" Joseph mumbled.

"I said: I have a package for you. You must sign for it."

"A package?"

"Yes, a package," the messenger set his pen and clipboard on the bed, so he could shine his gold buttons. "I just need your signature, then I'll be going. I have many other deliveries to make this morning. I'm always very busy this time of year."

Head still resting on the pillow, Joseph turned slowly and saw the dark silhouette of the messenger, standing over him, pen and clipboard poised. He could not see the messenger's face; the street lights seeping through the single window offered little illumination. But the buttons on the uniform shined like beacons, assuring him that a messenger was, in fact, before him. Only then did he catch a glimpse of the alarm clock.

"Does that say 3:00 am?" he asked excitedly, stirring in his bed. His irritation was obvious.

"Yes, of course it does," the messenger replied impatiently. "I keep odd hours. It's all part and parcel of the job. Please now," he reached over the bed and shook Joseph gently, "sign for the package, so I can be going."

"What is this package you keep going on about?" Joseph propped himself up, rubbing his eyes. "Are you sure you have the right apartment?"

"I never make mistakes," the messenger pushed the pen and clipboard against Joseph's chest. "If there ever is a mistake, it is the fault of the person receiving, not the person delivering."

"Well, if you'll leave me in peace," Joseph scratched down his signature, his head falling back down to the pillow. "Good night now," he pulled the covers up around himself.

"The package is on your desk," the messenger moved towards the open window. "The sooner you open it the better."

Out of curiosity, Joseph glanced at the desk. There was a rather large square package resting there. It was covered in an attractive silver wrap that, surprisingly, reflected the entire room around it. However, he was much too stubborn, and too upset at being inconvenienced at such an hour, to let on he had any genuine interest in it.

"Are you still awake over there?" the messenger suddenly interrupted his thoughts.

Joseph twisted around, seeing only the top of the messenger's head through the open window.

"You should open that package immediately." the messenger warned him, clutching the window sill to maintain his position, "and you should remember to keep this window closed; this time of year, you'll get a terrible draft - it'll make you sick!"

"I'll get right on it," Joseph twisted back, pulling on his covers. "Good night now."

Joseph heard a stirring in his landlady's apartment, next door. No doubt, she had an ear pressed against the wall. She was overly nosey, and the slightest hint of a stranger in anyone's apartment, especially at such an early hour, caused her great alarm. Tomorrow morning, she would probably threaten to raise his rent, on the account that his open window allowed heat to escape. With that in mind, and to prevent the arrival of another messenger, he threw back the covers, leaped up, ran over, and closed the window securely.

Climbing back into bed, pulling up the covers, he was confident there would be no further disturbances. He sighed deeply. There was so much on his mind, all relating to various aspects of work. However, the package also weighed heavy on his thoughts. He had to force himself not to look at it. The mere thought of it kept him awake. But his contempt for the messenger - for being awakened at such an hour - was so strong he steadfastly refused to accept both his advice and the package.

Joseph allowed facts and figures to swirl around in his head. The dizzying array lulled him to sleep, preparing him to dream up another idea to improve sales, an idea to make note of in the morning. Just as a profit margin appeared before him, he thought he heard someone knocking, but he couldn't be sure. The door to his apartment opened into the living room, which was separated from the bedroom by a thick wall and a heavy oak door. Thus, when in bed, he rarely heard callers. It was easy enough to pretend he heard nothing at all; that's how he'd approach the situation, considering he was perturbed at losing his train of thought. Besides, it was probably only his landlady, who felt obliged to deal with the issue of the open window immediately, rather than wait for a proper hour.

Sighing deeply, he pulled his covers up tight. He was slowly forgetting about the package, and the knocking, when he heard a terrible racket, just beyond his bedroom door. Sitting up in bed, clenching his blankets, he listened carefully. Could he be mistaken? Was his tired mind playing tricks on him? But the sound was unmistakable - repeated banging, splintering wood. The racket stopped, followed by the sound of several heavy footsteps rushing across the living room floor, approaching his bedroom door. He brought the covers up to his face. Where could he hide? There was no escape. The telephone was in the other room. He was completely helpless. These intruders - whoever they were, whatever they wanted - armed with axes, rushing towards his room, would have no contest. His bedroom door didn't even have a lock, to at least inconvenience their terrible mission - not that they bothered trying the door.

He jumped up three feet when the first blow struck, the axe blade stabbing right through the door. Blow after blow, splinters flew up. He could smell the oak, as the door disintegrated. He sat in awe - petrified by fear and helplessness. Surely his landlady would hear this and see fit to call the police, he thought - he hoped. He wished he was on better terms with her.

The door was reduced to a mere splintered frame of wood, almost off its hinges. The first figure rushed in, followed by three others. Joseph could not see them well, in the dim light and in his state of panic, but they all appeared to be wearing large hats and matching attire. He closed his eyes and prayed - something he rarely, if ever, did. The light on his desk clicked on. There was silence, but he knew they were all gathered around him, perhaps poised for the kill. He remained motionless, holding his breath, hoping they couldn't sense his fear. But nothing happened - no movement, no sound. Slowly, reluctantly, he opened his eyes. There were four firemen gathered around his bed.

"So there you are," one with a clipboard smiled, seating himself right next to Joseph. "You're in bed."

"Yes," Joseph replied, still shaken, "that's where I can be found at 3 o'clock in the morning."

"What an effort," another fireman sighed, setting down his axe. The other two, at the foot of the bed with their axes, nodded in agreement. "We had some trouble getting through to you," he continued, wiping his brow. "Not that this place is too big - far from it - but those doors presented a problem initially, especially the heavy oak one."

"It's all part of your job," the one with the clipboard began, shining his badge, as if to remind everyone he was the chief. "You can expect a lot of this kind of thing, during this time of year. Now, go see what he has in the refrigerator."

The two firemen at the foot of the bed set down their axes and ran to inspect the kitchen. The other seated himself at the desk and, noticing the package sitting there, immediately informed the chief.

"So," the fire chief slapped Joseph on the knee, "I see you've got your package."

"Yes, it's true," Joseph replied.

"You don't seem too excited," the fire chief looked at him curiously. "That's a bad sign."

"How can I be excited about anything right now?" Joseph suddenly burst. "This is the second interruption I've had this evening! I'm beginning to wonder if I'll ever be allowed to sleep in peace!"

"My friend," the fire chief began in defence, "keep in mind the time of year, and the importance of your package. Notice how the package reflects everything around you. It's special, and it was delivered to you for a reason. It is of the utmost significance because ..."

"No," Joseph snapped, not allowing him to continue, "I won't listen. I've got work to keep in mind, duties to perform and promises to keep. I need a good night's sleep to accomplish these things, unlike you bunch, who seem to shirk your proper responsibilities so you can go visiting people at odd hours. Why aren't you out fighting fires?" he sat up, emphasizing his displeasure. "Surely with all the lights and ornaments the entire city should be ablaze!"

The fire chief shook his head.

"Isn't it worth your time to look at it?" he leaned in towards Joseph. "Don't you want to find out what's inside?"

"I couldn't care less," Joseph threw his arms up. "I've already explained my situation, and I think I've been more than patient throughout all of this. Just count yourself lucky I'm not on the telephone pressing charges against all of you! Now please, I'm only going to say this once more, leave me alone so I can sleep!"

The two firemen returned from inspecting the kitchen.

"He's got next to nothing in his refrigerator," one announced, as if surprised.

"He doesn't even have coffee made," the other complained.

The fire chief turned to Joseph, looking him up and down.

"You're not much of a host."

He got up from the bed and led the other three firemen out the door.

Joseph let out yet another sigh - something he was getting good at. He was glad to finally see them go, since they made such a nuisance of themselves, and the fire chief was sitting on his leg. As the firemen made their way out, he heard them stop in the hallway to talk to his landlady, who was probably listening all along. With no doors to conceal secrets, he could hear everything being said.

"Is he dead?" the landlady asked.

Joseph could hardly keep himself from laughing out loud at her odd question.

"Stupid old woman," he thought, smiling, "so paranoid and nosey. Always having to know who was coming and going. Always having to know which tenants were dead and which ones were alive!"

"Well," the fire chief paused. Joseph found this curious. He listened carefully; it seemed the fire chief was actually taking her question seriously!

"He is, isn't he?" the landlady pressed on.

"In a manner of speaking, yes."

Joseph listened to footsteps disappearing down the hallway. Now that he was completely alone, he did not know what to think about the exchange between the fire chief and the landlady; he certainly didn't find it at all amusing. He found himself thinking up convenient excuses. Perhaps he was too tired, and did not hear their conversation correctly. Perhaps they rehearsed the entire incident - messenger, package, firemen and all - in an effort to scare him, to make him more agreeable about the management of the apartment building. At any rate, it made no difference to him. There was too much else on his mind. He simply had to get some sleep, if he was going to complete the various work-related tasks coursing through his head. More importantly, he would never agree with the management of the apartment building. He actually considered ways to manage it more efficiently with fewer costs - should he ever have control of it.

Satisfied with his own understanding of things, and convinced he could not be defeated, he prepared for sleep. He caught a brief glimpse of the square package, still on his desk, untouched, its silver packaging reflecting everything around him. It would remain there forever, he thought, until the landlady, or whoever else was responsible, finally gave in, admitted it was all just a prank, and took the accursed thing away. The thought that someone else was responsible, other than the landlady, greatly appealed to him. It made good sense; he was very successful at work and he often thought the other workers were jealous of him. It wouldn't take much effort to arrange the entire charade - hire a messenger, call the fire department - in an attempt at tiring him out, so he wasn't as productive. Then again, maybe they just wanted to discredit him altogether. Regardless, it would never work. He would never fall prey to such underhanded tactics. Comfortable with these thoughts, sleep came quickly.

Visions of facts and figures once again filled his head. He always had such neatly organized and well-presented dreams. Everything appeared in brilliantly coloured pie charts and easily interpreted tables. The statistics were indisputable. A spreadsheet of future forecasts was about to come off the printer, when he was rudely awakened. It took him awhile to realize his blankets had been pulled away. The desk lamp was on, blinding his tired eyes. Squinting, he saw the maid folding up his blankets.

"What are you up to?" he demanded to know, "Can't this wait until I've left for work, or at least gotten out of bed?"

"The landlady sent me up," she replied, in her usual stoic manner. "She wants all your linen changed. Besides," she pulled the pillow out from beneath him, causing his head to strike the wooden headboard, "you left your door open."

"Door?" Joseph rubbed his head. "What door? There are no doors to speak of! I'm beginning to think I'm better off sleeping in a barn full of animals!"

"It's a real shock to everyone in the building," she said, quite out of the blue, folding his pillowcase.

"What's that?" Joseph looked at her with amazement now.

"That you're dead. Some people were actually rather fond of you."

"That's it," he leaped out of bed, just as she was trying to pull the bedspread out from beneath him, "I've really had enough of this craziness. I've finally had it." He bolted to his closet, pulling his trench coat over his pyjamas. "Since I'm not permitted to sleep, due to either unrelated circumstances conspiring against me or a genuine set up, I'm going for a walk - with all the other dead people in the city! When I get back," he whipped on some socks and shoes, "I expect everything to be in order, including the mess that was made of my doors. And I demand I be allowed to sleep for at least a few hours before work!"

"Don't forget your package," the maid neatly folded his bedspread, as he made his way towards the bedroom door. "It's the most valuable thing you possess. It shouldn't leave your sight."

"Good night," he growled, tired of hearing about the package. However, he could not help looking at it as he went by, briefly catching a glimpse of himself in it. He almost stopped, somewhat fascinated, although he would not admit to it - that would be admitting defeat. Besides, why should he follow the advice of a common worker who doesn't even have enough sense to wait for a person to leave his bed before changing the linen?

Leaving the apartment, heading down the hall, his curiosity about the package somewhat diminished his feelings of anger. Now that he was practically wide awake, he gained a new perspective on the subject. It struck him that the package, and the events surrounding its arrival, seemed too complex to be a mere prank. Too many people were involved, from maids to firemen. It didn't make sense: why would someone go through all that trouble just to get at him? There was now, he believed, no convenient excuse for the evening's events. He would have to take everything at face value; in which case, he had to deny his own curiosity, because the package already consumed too much of his time and energy. Regardless, he would not admit defeat. His position remained firm. His refusal to open the package, or pay any real attention to it, was both an affirmation that he was better off without it and a highly significant gesture of passive aggression to all those who interfered with his morning.

Joseph passed through the front doors of the apartment building. His eyes remained fixed on the sidewalk unfolding beneath his steps. The cool air was a welcome change. It cleared his head of all the nonsense, allowing concentration on more important business-related matters. Sleep was pretty much out of the question. He now considered a brief walk before preparing to leave for work - earlier than usual. It would be beneficial to arrive early. He could make use of various facilities that were normally booked solid for the day - providing anyone else would actually show up during the holidays. Confident with this new plan of action, he felt that the package, and all events related to it, could hardly faze him at all. Smiling to himself, he looked up from the sidewalk. He stopped dead in his tracks. At that moment, all thoughts escaped him. Fear flooded in, filling the void. Fear: the first reaction when the senses dull and one can no longer find his way. But when the senses adjust, quite quickly in some cases, ignorance recedes, understanding begins, and the lightness in the stomach disappears.

Briefly, he floundered in a sea of churning gray. It drowned the night air, taking everything else down with it. Calming himself, he felt stupid for having known nothing about it. Yet it was, after all, highly uncommon for that time of year. It was undoubtedly the sort of thing keeping families indoors, gathered around their trees; keeping carollers practicing in well-lit churches, rather than venturing to doorsteps. It was only the speed he immersed himself that caught him off guard. It was perhaps more distressing that all things familiar disappeared. Although he was directly in front of the apartment building, there were no lights. Blinded, he stumbled into something. But he had yet to move from his spot. Something had stumbled into him.

Joseph apologized. The person said nothing. Somehow, Joseph did not hear him approaching, causing him some embarrassment. Perhaps he was just too distracted by it all - not to mention too tired. The person kept on walking - just another restless soul on an early morning walk, trapped in the fog, just like Joseph. It was obviously a ridiculous idea - walking in such weather. The fog seemed to be thickening; he didn't know how anyone else could tolerate it. Turning to head back into the apartment building, considering breakfast before leaving for work, he had to restrain himself from crying out.

"My God," he gasped, laughing nervously, "You nearly scared me to death!"

The man said nothing. Joseph had no idea the man was behind him; he could have been there all along. Regardless, now they were face to face. The man had pale, expressionless features. His hands sank deep into the pockets of his dark trench coat. Without a sound, no acknowledgment whatsoever, he walked away, disappearing into the fog. Joseph shook his head. Such a strange morning, and it was beginning to take its toll on him. He could not wait to get back to his apartment, surely a mere ten paces away - easily accomplished, even in such dense fog. He returned to contemplating the best possible breakfast. But the firemen were right: there was next to nothing in his refrigerator.

Moving towards the front doors, he caught himself thinking of the package. His curiosity was still quite great. Figuring that the maid was finished in his apartment, he made up his mind to open it. No one would see him do it, so he wouldn't be openly admitting to any kind of weakness. Perhaps more importantly, he wouldn't have to respect poor advice given by suspicious early morning visitors. It would be simple: if the contents proved to be useless, or a prank, he'd throw it all out. After all, if it remained unopened on his desk, it would only distract him from his work, which may be the intentions of all those conspiring against him.

Satisfied with his plan, and allowing himself to be distracted by various other thoughts, he continued towards the front doors. He could not recall venturing quite so far away from them. Walking a few more paces, he reached out, expecting to touch some of the ornamental shrubs decorating the front. He found nothing. Was he still too far off? It was not possible, he thought. Even if he had not turned straight towards the doors, surely he should run into a neighbouring railing, shrubbery, or wall. He silently cursed his virtual blindness. He felt more frustrated than afraid. How could he get lost right outside his own apartment building?

"Oh," he blurted, turning his head. Someone brushed against him. "Sorry, but I'm a bit disorientated," he laughed nervously; "could you direct me towards my apartment building - it's the Johnston Building, 3201 Maple Street."

The stranger, oblivious to Joseph's request, disappeared into the fog. The stranger looked, and acted, much like the others. Joseph wondered if he was running into the exact same person each time. However, that seemed improbable. A group of three such men, all walking close together, shoulders touching, brushed by him. He saw the same pale, expressionless faces, and the same dark trench coats. Being an organized, reasonable type, he wouldn't let it get the best of him; but he was genuinely worried. Right within his own city, he felt very alone and uncomfortable. He picked up the pace. He was at a complete loss to find his apartment building, let alone any building at all.

"Where are they coming from?" he wondered aloud.

He could hardly avoid bumping into them. Who were they and what was their excuse for being out in such weather? It was useless to question them. They were completely unaware of everything around them. He panicked. He would have knocked a few of them over, if they weren't so stiff, almost immovable. Where was he running? Where could he go? To run face first into a building - anything other than them - would be a relief.

"There you are!" a strangely familiar voice called out.

Joseph tried to catch his breath. He was desperate to talk, to say anything to this welcome passer-by. The shock and excitement at hearing a voice - a familiar one, at that - was too much for him to bare.

"I didn't think I'd ever find you at your new address," the voice drew closer, "but then again, regardless of the weather, it's all part and parcel of the job."

Joseph recognized the voice. Seeing the silhouette, the shining gold buttons, he immediately knew who was approaching.

"The messenger?" he gasped, hands on knees, still trying to recover.

"You left this back at your apartment," the messenger remained somewhat hidden in the fog. "I see you didn't open it.

That's a bad sign. But then again, it's no fault of mine. If there is ever a mistake, it is the fault of the person receiving, not the person delivering."

The messenger stood silently, with the silver package resting in his outstretched hands.

"Why is this package so important?" Joseph wiped his brow. "What's in it that's so valuable that my entire morning has been compromised because of it? What's in it that causes you more concern than my being trapped in this terrible fog?"

"It's not that simple," the messenger explained. "You're the only one who knows what the package contains. The package is meant for you alone. It is of significance to you alone. In a manner of speaking, it contains everything that you truly are, or truly could be, instead of that which you appear to be."

The messenger pushed the package against Joseph's chest.

"Sorry to be impatient," the messenger smiled, "but I have many other deliveries to make this morning. I'm always very busy this time of year."

Joseph grasped the package.

"There's no need for you to sign for it now," the messenger said.

The messenger vanished into the fog. Joseph was alone with his package. The messenger's abrupt, seemingly uncaring manner, made him somewhat upset. His attention quickly turned to what was at hand. The package, its surface still shimmering, seemed unable to catch his reflection, no matter how close he pressed his face to it. It was a disturbing effect, probably caused by the dense fog, he thought. Without further hesitation, or any better plan of action, he tore open the silver wrap. He peered inside the box and shook it. Looking up, he hoped to speak to the messenger about the mistake. He shook the box again, feeling its inside corners. As a final test, he turned it upside down. A joke, he thought - undoubtedly. Throwing the remains of the package to the ground, he continued walking in no particular direction, with no particular destination in mind.

ABOUT THE AUTHOR

Cameron A. Straughan is a writer, photographer, film maker and teacher of science. His writing has appeared in several popular publications including 'Satire: The Journal of Contemporary Satire', 'The Dream People Online Literary Journal' and 'Black Cat 115'. He has performed his short stories at several open-mike events; including readings in Windsor, Ontario, and throughout Vancouver, BC. His award-winning humorous films have appeared in many festivals around the world. His play "Bear Mask" will soon be produced in London, UK.

www.ingramcontent.com/pod-product-compliance
Lightning Source LLC
Chambersburg PA
CBHW020619130626
46552CB00003B/1045